The Moon and the Night

The Moon and the Night

Sarah Birdsall

A Northern Nights Book
Northern Nights Press
Talkeetna, Alaska

Published in Talkeetna, Alaska, by Northern Nights Press.

This is a work of fiction. Any resemblance to persons living or dead is coincidental.

Originally published in 2013 as a Kindle E-book under the pseudonym Sarah Somebody

ISBN 979-8-218-22168-3

To my daughter, Jenny, and all her Talkeetna friends, who always spent many hours reading and reading and reading, and to the memory of Marsha Mak, who was this book's first fan.

The Moon and
the Night

Prologue

Tri is for Trileka is for try, Trileka, try.

I thought this that night, that awful night, as I drug Ethan, half-naked and bleeding, through the dark woods. *Try, Trileka, try.* A chant from my childhood. Something familiar. Something that made me feel like somehow, I was going to get through this.

Ethan groaned and swayed against me. I could hear dogs barking in the woods behind us. We were leaving a bloody trail in the snow. "Come on," I whispered. *"Come on."* I could see, even in the blue-black dark, his face twisting with pain as he pulled his mangled foot forward.

Try, Trileka, try.

I thought of my sister, Su, short for Susitna, one blue eye, one brown. We were named for mountains. I thought of our stepmother, Winter. Winter Wolf. Named for winter.

And named for wolves. But I did not know that then.

The cold was biting. Ethan would freeze. I didn't know—I couldn't imagine—what had happened to his clothes.

I had seen something. There was a wolf, then there was Ethan. Wolf, Ethan.

My arms ached. I nearly tripped on an icy, slippery root, nearly fell and nearly took Ethan with me. He was losing a lot of blood. Could he die? Then I saw the light of home in the trees.

It had been less than two weeks since Ethan came into our lives. But in that moment I knew it was a whole world ago.

One

I get up first, in our house. I get the fire going, get the coffee going, put on the water for a pot of oatmeal and let our dog, Keats, outside. I hit the bathroom, then I wake up Su, and she snarls at me before slamming the bathroom door. I get dressed in our small, shared room, brush out the wavy brown hair that falls to my waist, do a quick check in the mirror then run downstairs to finish the oatmeal and pack the lunches and let Keats back in. When Su comes down, I make sure she remembers to put her homework in her backpack; I shove a bowl of oatmeal at her and tell her to hurry up and eat. If it's cold outside, I go start the Subaru wagon we've had since before our dad died. Then I go upstairs and wake Winter, hand her a sweater to pull on over her long-johns, escort her down the stairs. I grab the lunches, then we rush out the door to drive to the bus stop, no one but me knowing our clock is set five minutes ahead—always.

That is the morning routine, and the mid-October day we first learned of Ethan Monroe seemed no different, just another number on the calendar passing into history.

"Winter, we'll miss the bus," I said as we stood outside by the old blue Subie with its chipped paint and rusty patches. She was looking at the dark ceiling of sky, feeling the slight wind. It would be a gray day. I was thinking it might snow.

"No," she said, as she got into the driver's seat, maneuvering coffee cup, seat belt and car keys. "No snow today. Not yet. Tonight or tomorrow." We already had about three inches on the ground from earlier in the month. The weather, this year, was not messing around.

I looked at Su in the backseat and we exchanged a glance, our unspoken words saying, Yeah, she's weird. I kept my eye on Su until she clicked her seatbelt and glared at me with some irritation. I was about to say something about her dark eyeliner (how had I missed that?) then thought better of it. Su was fourteen, and she was tired of me hovering over her, not to mention the fact that her moods were becoming as dark as her shiny, near pitch black hair.

"Winter—road," I said as the car swerved into the oncoming lane after we left our narrow dirt drive.

"Oops," Winter said, twisting the wheel. "Thanks, Tri." Six years ago our dad disappeared in his small plane that crashed somewhere in a nearby mountain range, and I'd been riding shotgun ever since: one eye on Su, one eye on Winter and whatever we were heading toward.

The road to our house was wider than our drive, but it was loosely graveled and full of ruts. The early winter woods stretched out on either side—barren trees, bent brown grasses sticking up out of the snow. The occasional surviving cranberry stood out, blood red amidst all the brown and white. But this morning it was still too dark to see all this. The dark was coming, and it wouldn't be long before it would not only be dark when we left for school, but near dark before we even made it back home.

I reached down and turned on the radio. The local station was the only one we could get; everything else was too far away—other towns, other stations. The voice of our Aunt Tabby's boyfriend, Sydney, came over the airwaves in the Australian accent that reminded me and Su there was a world beyond our tiny town:

". . .there's no snow in the forecast yet, loves, but there's a fresh dusting in the higher elevations, so we're bound to get a little more of the white stuff sooner rather than later. . ."

Winter muttered something, taking a wide turn on the way down the steeply graded hill that led to the paved road below. I took a silent, deep breath; thankfully no one was coming the other way. I was working on getting my driver's license; Sydney was teaching me, but our schedules didn't often match so it was going slow. Our bus stop was three miles from where we lived; our school was another fifteen. So for now Su and I were dependent on Winter to get us there.

I looked both ways with Winter as we turned out onto the paved road, then took a quick glance back at her: I saw a little gray in her shoulder length black hair. It startled me. Winter wasn't very old, and it didn't seem that long ago that she'd married our dad, but as I thought about it I realized that was ten years ago, when I was six and Su was four, and we'd been without our mom for three years. No—she didn't die, our mother. She merely left us and vanished into the world.

The bus pulled up out of the twilight gray of the morning shortly after we'd reached the stop. Su and I climbed aboard and while she slunk toward an empty seat in the middle I sat near the front of the bus, like I always did, my head turned away from, but my ears not closed to, the happy ruckus of the popular kids sitting in the back.

The back was where Chris Evans sat, a boy I rode the bus with five mornings and five afternoons a week, every week of the school year: a boy who never seemed to see me. And why should he, I thought: Chris lived in a different world, a bright and sunny world, a world with two parents and a nice house and plenty of friends. A world that seemed to glow like the lighted windows of a happy home, while I stood on the dark side of the glass. So I'd been making it a point to stop seeing him, and to stop imagining a world where I was visible, where he said hello to me, where he sat by me on the bus, where one fine day he asked me out. It wasn't going to happen.

"And how are the Tyler girls?" Mr. Palmer, the bus driver, asked. He was balding and overweight, and always nice—not just to me, but to kids who looked down their noses at him and who didn't deserve to have him give them the time of day.

"We're fine," I said.

"Another day," he said.

"Yep."

"Another day in history."

"Yep." Mr. Palmer knew I wanted to be a historian. He was always reminding me that tomorrow's history was happening right now, so we'd better pay attention to it. And I would—pay attention. Because I believed him, because it made me feel better, somehow, about everything that happened—and didn't happen—in my life, to place it in the context of history-in-the-making, to recognize that what was insignificant today might be significant when seen through the lens of time, and that what was significant today might be of little consequence in the big picture of all the things the years would bring.

I thought about this when I thought of Chris Evans and how I knew he would never like me. I thought about this when Winter would be late for a parent-teacher-student-conference. I thought about this every year when first Mother's Day and then Father's Day rolled around.

A wash of yellowish light broke through the darkness as, after a half-hour bus ride, we arrived at River Valley Jr./Sr. High School. Emma, my best and it seemed only friend, was waiting for me: her mother worked at the school, so she was spared having to ride one of the buses, which brought kids to the school from three different directions. It was the only high school for miles, and it was built on a plot of land near a lonely stretch of highway that ran north and south across the center of Alaska. The nearest town of significance was an hour's drive south; up north there were a number of small villages and towns scattered along the highway, but you'd have to drive six hours to come upon anything resembling a city.

"Did he acknowledge your existence?" Emma asked, watching Chris Evans come off the bus.

"Emma," I said, a warning in my voice. I didn't want to talk about Chris Evans anymore.

"He's stupid," she said. Emma was only as tall as me but she was thin and because of that looked taller and pixie-like, her short curly blond hair adding to the effect.

I shook my head. "You know he's not."

"I can think so if I want."

"Think away then," I said. We went inside, and Chris Evans nearly bumped into us as he rushed past us in the hall, as if he couldn't see we were even there. And so I started my school day, which passed slowly and without consequence.

Later, on the bus ride home, I tried to enjoy the fact that it was still light outside and sat with my head against the cool window watching the miles pass: miles of trees mostly, birches in varying shades of gray and the dark somberly green spruce. Soon so much would be buried in snow. Snow that would last and last and last, sometimes until the middle of May.

As our bus neared our stop Su, in a seat behind me, said, "Winter's not there."

That was nothing new. "She'll come. We can walk a ways."

"No, I mean, Sydney's there."

I straightened in my seat and looked out the window. Sydney stood beside his battered off-white truck, his longish blond hair in a short sloppy ponytail and a buffalo plaid wool coat that looked too big for him hanging off his shoulders.

Su looked at me, wonder in her eyes.

"I'm sure everything's fine," I said.

"Girls!" Sydney said as we stepped off. "I've come to get you!"

"What's going on?" I asked.

"Well, Winter had to take a bit of a drive, I guess. Her nephew's flying in, and she had to go to Anchorage to pick him up. So I'm supposed to pick you up and take you into town." He smiled.

Su and I looked at each other. Of Winter's relatives, we'd only met her parents. And that was only once. They were both tall and angular looking, with the same black hair and brown-black eyes that Winter had. But unlike Winter, they weren't warm and fuzzy.

"Winter never said she had a nephew," I said.

"I really don't know much about it, girls, I'm just following my orders."

"Where's Aunt Tabby?" I asked. We walked over to his pick-up.

"Oh, at T2—where else?" T2 Air, the family business, my dad's dream. Aunt Tabby kept it going; why, we weren't sure: she didn't even really like to fly and T2 certainly wasn't my dream—or Su's (though Su did have aviation related ambitions; she wanted to be a stewardess). Neither of us had plans to stay in our miniscule village near the massive Alaska Range after we graduated from high school.

"Why don't you just take us home?" I asked. Su and I could certainly manage on our own.

"Well, it's something about Winter wanting to get Ethan settled in before you girls got home," Sydney said.

Again, Su and I looked at each other. "Is there something wrong with him?" I asked.

"Not that I'm aware of, girls."

"Did you know about him?"

"Me? Nah—I'm out of many loops."

"Did Tabby?"

"She seems to."

"So does Winter have a brother or a sister?"

"Come again?"

"If Ethan's her nephew, does she have a brother or a sister?"

"Oh, right—sister, I think. But I'm not sure on that."

"How old is he?" Su asked.

"Well, actually, I think he's just a tad bit older than you girls."

"Is he going to go to school?" I asked.

"Oh I think so—if they'll let him in and all that." Then Sydney grimaced, as if he'd said something he shouldn't have.

"Why wouldn't they let him in?" I asked, then quickly added, "So there is something wrong with him."

"No, not really. Just your usual Rebel Without a Cause thing, girls."

"What's that?" Su asked.

"Rebel Without a Cause? That's a movie, Su, and one I think you in particular might be able to relate to. But basically, I think he—Ethan—just got in some teen-angst type trouble and was sent up here to let old Auntie Winter straighten him out."

"Great," I said. Winter could barely take care of us. How would she "straighten out" someone else?

Sydney caught my tone. "It'll be all right, Tri. You and Su come first. If this doesn't work out, old Ethan will be put on the first plane out of here."

"To where?"

"Canada, I think."

"How in the world does Winter have family in Canada?" I asked, but Sydney only shrugged.

Aunt Tabby was on the phone and standing behind a cluttered counter when we walked in. She raised a hand in our direction, and Su and I found a table and pulled our homework out of our backpacks. The T2 office was our second home, and we were well used to it.

"Snacks?" Tabby asked, her phone call finished. She pushed her puffy sandy colored hair away from her delicate-featured face.

Su nodded, but I said, "Can't we just go home?"

Tabby shook her head. "Just hang in there with us a bit. Winter will be back soon."

"So what's the big secret anyway?"

"Big secret? Tri, honey, there's no secret."

"And does Winter have a brother or a sister?"

"A sister."

"How come we never met her—and how come we never met him?"

Tabby shrugged. "I don't know—she's some kind of a biologist and had been working and living pretty remotely for quite a while."

"In Canada."

Tabby shot Sydney a look. "Yes, in Canada."

"I would have thought Winter would have told us." I looked away. I could feel the effect of my tone cross Tabby's face. Su was looking at me, her brown eye and her blue eye both filled with a look that made me regret my words. She was leveraging the situation, assessing if there was reason to, once we got home, shut herself up in our room with her earbuds in and Nirvana on her iPod. I took a deep breath and said, trying to force a different attitude into my voice, "Well, I'm sure she has her reasons."

"So, are you girls hungry?" Tabby asked.

Su nodded slightly, her eyes still sliding about warily. I knew she was hungry—she was always hungry these days—but she hated to seem too eager about anything.

"Granola bars and juice?"

Su made a face. "Do you have anything else?"

"Su—" I said. Lately she seemed to only want to eat meat; when I'd said something to Winter, she'd said something about teenage hormones. I couldn't remember ever having those kinds of hormones.

Tabby smiled. "Jerky?"

Su licked her lips, her blunt, short black hair shiny and glossy: shinier than mine. Blacker than mine. And beautifully straight. Her face was noticeably slimmer and not as round as mine, but at least my nose was smaller than hers—not as wide at the base.

"Tri?" Tabby asked, about the jerky.

"No, thanks," I said, pulling out my paperback copy of Shakespeare's tragedies. We were reading Macbeth in drama class. I had other homework, but this would suit my mood.

By the prickling of my thumbs, something wicked this way comes.

. .

I thought of those words, from the play, and felt a strange sensation on the back of my neck. What was coming our way?

☾

It wasn't until nine o'clock or so that night that Sydney and Tabby drove us home under a starless, moonless sky that left the thick woods around where we lived in dense darkness. There was a chill in the air that foreshadowed the deep winter soon to come, and when I hopped out of the crowded cab of the pickup and my feet hit the friendly ground of the familiar drive, I looked at the rough-hewn house my father had built and my mother had abandoned, at its wooden walls and steep-pitched roofs and glowing yellow windows and saw a strange form pass through the light inside.

Two

The arctic entryway was dark and smelled of dog. "Keats?" I asked, but he was nowhere to be seen. Then my boot hit something soft under the bench. I bent down and looked. There was Keats—a big Shepard-mixed mutt—squeezed into the low space, pressed against the wall. He looked at me with worried eyes but gave a teeny wag of his tail. I thought of Su outside, coming in behind me with Tabby and Sydney.

"It's okay, Keats," I said, then hurried in through the heavy wooden door.

To my left was the kitchen, which I could see was empty. In front of me, to the side of the wooden staircase, a narrow hall led to the back door. I had a strange feeling that door had just closed. I looked to my right; Winter was in the living area by the fire, sitting in my dad's old recliner which had been patched up with corduroy over the years. She looked calm and smiled when she saw me.

"Tri! How was school?"

I didn't waste any time. "Where's your nephew?" I asked.

"Ethan? Oh—he's staying in one of the guest cabins."

Since my dad's death we made our living by renting out three small guest cabins toward the back of our house. It was good money in the summer, but not so good in the winter.

I looked quickly around. I knew I had seen someone pass in front of one of the windows—someone who wasn't Winter. He *had* gone out the back door, then, just as we arrived. Why?

"He's not feeling good," Winter said, as if she could read my mind. "Tri, what is it?"

I could hear the others in the entryway. "You just never told us about him," I said. "And now Tabby says he's going to live here. What if we don't like him?"

"You'll like him," she said.

"You can't know that." My eyes fell on a picture of my dad, near where I stood. My dad and me and Su. "This is still our house," I said quickly. "You should have asked me and Su."

I saw the sting of my words in Winter's brown-black eyes. "You're right, Tri—I'm sorry. It just happened very fast. But he is my family. I couldn't turn him away."

I left the living room as the others filtered in.

Upstairs, I kept the light off in my room and pulled my chair over to the window. The night was dark and quiet, and it took me awhile to discern any shapes in all that blackness. I looked toward where the guest cabins were and wondered which one she'd put him in. I guessed the first one, but there were no lights on in any of them. Was he sleeping already? And then a thought came to me, one that made my skin tingle. Could he be, like me, sitting in a dark window, looking out? Looking at the house, at us—at the scene framed in the lighted window of the kitchen downstairs. It was only a thought, but somehow I felt that it was true. I pulled my curtain closed and lifted the edge just enough to peek out. I concentrated on the windows of the first cabin, which I could only identify because the light from the house stretched in that direction, allowing me to barely be able to separate window from wall. If only the moon, which I'd seen the night before hanging low and orange yellow in the sky, weren't covered by clouds. I thought about poor Keats, huddled in the entryway. What was he afraid of? My dad had always said, about himself: "Animals and kids—well, they like me so I must be okay." If Keats was afraid of Ethan, what did that mean?

My eyes hurt from staring at the dark. Then I saw it, and I knew I'd been right: a flash of movement, whitish like pale skin or how you'd think a ghost might look, in one of the downstairs windows of the first guest cabin.

He was watching us.

"My family hasn't always gotten along," Winter said in the morning. We were in the kitchen, Winter up early for once, and Su was in the bathroom, taking a hurried shower. Ethan, Winter said, wasn't feeling well and would not be going to school that day. "My sister—my sister isn't like me. We believe in different things. We're not like you and Su, Tri. We're different."

"But what about *him*?" I nodded my head toward the wall that faced the back of the house, toward the guest cabin. "Is he different, too?"

"He's just a kid. Like you."

"Like me," I said. A kid. I could almost laugh at that; I couldn't remember when I'd last felt like a "kid." I said, rising from the table, "Your coffee's done; Su's oatmeal is on the stove. I'll go start the car."

"Tri—" But I had already left the room.

It was the same story again, when we got home from school: Ethan wasn't feeling well. Su took it in stride at first, but I could see her glancing over at the guest cabin as we fetched armfuls of wood from the woodshed. The day was gray and warm—just above freezing—and the ground was coated with a new inch of soggy snow that had fallen during the afternoon. Even though fall was long gone (fall was September), the air still smelled of cranberries and dead leaves and the woods looked barren and bleak despite the recent snow, which brightened things a little. I noticed two black and white magpies flitting in and out of the trees.

"What do you think he's doing in there?" Su whispered as I piled wood into her arms. She glanced again toward the guest cabin.

"I have no idea," I said.

"What do you think's wrong with him?" Su asked.

"I don't know. Probably nothing."

"But why can't we even meet him?"

"Maybe it's like Winter says."

"It's just kind of weird, don't you think?"

"Well," I said, "he is related to Winter."

"That is a fact," she said, with a hint of a smile.

"Yes," I said, and we let it go at that, for the moment.

$$\mathcal{D}$$

We didn't meet Ethan that night, nor did we meet him the next day. It wasn't until the day after that, as we hurried out the door to catch the bus, that Winter casually said, "So—I'll be coming out to the school later, to register Ethan."

Su and I stopped and looked at her. We'd given up, these last couple of days, on trying to get anything out of Winter about Ethan and we'd decided to act like we just didn't care.

But I could feel him out there, almost as if I could see him in the windows he magically avoided during the daylight hours. And Keats was jumpy and jittery and paced the floors at night.

Emma wasn't waiting for me when the bus arrived at school that day; she sent our little friend, Jack-the-Freshman, to greet me.

"Parent problems?" I asked Jack as he walked up to me.

He nodded. Emma's mother, who was a teacher at the school, tended to blame me anytime she felt dissatisfied with Emma, and she felt dissatisfied with her often. Emma wasn't turning out how her parents thought she should. Since I was Emma's first friend after the family moved here from Oregon three years ago, and since my family wasn't "normal," they naturally thought Emma's occasionally eccentric behavior had something to do with me.

"Her mom will be watching the halls today," Jack said. That meant watching us—me and Emma.

"Thank you, Jack," I said. Jack nodded and walked back toward the school, hands in the pockets of his jeans and shoulders hunched against the cold. Jack always wore a ski hat—the kind with little flaps by the ears—and I watched its bright pattern slip through the glass and metal doors. Su came up beside me. "Mrs. Fitch getting weird again?" she asked.

I nodded.

"Poor Emma," Su said.

I nodded again.

"Do you think Winter will really bring him?"

I watched Chris Evans walk into the school. "I don't know," I said. "I guess we'll find out."

"I think she will," Su said. "I have a feeling."

"She will or she won't," I said. Then the bell rang.

After lunch I was straightening out my locker when I began to feel strange. I was prickly all over, and everything felt so *close*: every wall, every smell, every movement of air—as if I'd been sleeping and was suddenly awake and aware of my surroundings for the first time. Then I felt something else, something new. Him. I *felt* him before I saw him, knew completely that he was there. I quickly turned my head.

He was at the end of the line of lockers, looking at me: a thin pale face with dark curling hair and big dark eyes that I could feel cutting through the distance between us— someone I had never seen before but in that moment felt known to me. And the air suddenly seemed thick and dense and full of smells—so many smells I felt choked by them, until overriding it all I could smell him, the dark-haired boy who was staring at me, musky and warm and strangely familiar and I had a vision then, of something—trees and snow. A jagged piece of sky. Then suddenly he was gone and the hall smelled like—well, like school: carpet cleaner, books, teenage sweat, and perfume. The bell had rung and the hall was swarming with activity.

Then there was Su, slipping up next to me. "He's here," she said.

"I saw."

"I told you she'd bring him."

"You had a fifty percent chance of being right."

"Well I was." She met my eyes. "He looks kind of cute," she said out of the corner of her mouth.

"Don't get any ideas," I said. "He's family."

"He is?"

"Just ask Winter." I slammed my locker closed and headed for class. On the way there a voice behind me said, "It is better to die standing than to live on your knees."

It was Jack, delivering a message from Emma.

"I hope she didn't say that in front of her mother," I said.

"Why?" he asked.

"It's Che Guevara. The Cuban revolutionary. From *The Motorcycle Diaries.*"

"Oh," Jack said, nodding. He was going to file that one away, I could tell.

We had algebra next, and I would get to see Emma. She sat silently several rows behind me; I tried to focus on her without focusing on her (the algebra teacher might be an informant for her mother, we'd decided), but I was sharply aware of another presence in the school. Every time someone moved I flinched; every time I heard footsteps in the hall I expected the door to open and *him* to be there. But he wasn't. Toward the end of the hour I began to relax.

After algebra, I parted with Jack and went to drama—Emma keeping a safe distance behind me. Drama was one of my favorite classes. Not that I liked acting—I didn't—but I loved reading the plays, loved how some of the plays were written so long ago, like a window into what that life was like—how people thought and what to them was funny or sad. We'd gone from reading the plays of Socrates and

Aristotle and were now on Shakespeare.

"The true revolutionary is guided by great feelings of love," Emma said as she slid past me toward a desk in the back. We felt relatively safe in this class; the teacher was someone we felt liked us. I started to turn to signal to Emma but then I felt something again, something on the back of my neck. I knew he had entered the room. I saw, too, on Emma's face that he had. I heard my heart in my ears. He passed by my desk just as my face lifted and our eyes met for an instant before he sat in a lone corner by the back wall. Emma looked at me, mouthed something. I still heard my heart, a swishing rhythm, and I could *smell* him as if my nose was buried in his skin.

How was this possible?

Ms. Curtis, the teacher, was saying something. The words seemed to swim through the air: ". . .we have a new student, his name is Ethan. Ethan lives with Trileka. Welcome, Ethan." While everyone looked at me and looked at him, he and I looked at each other.

After class he approached me as I waited with a pounding heart. "Trileka," he said.

"Tri," I said.

He nodded his head toward me, like a bow. Emma was lingering, risking her mother's wrath, and I could almost feel her sigh at the strange little gesture. "I didn't know about you," he said. His clothes were clean but worn and seemed to hang a little on his thin frame. Where his shirt sleeves were pushed up I could see his forearms, lean and muscular, with fine dark hairs on his light skin.

"I didn't know about you, either," I said. Our eyes met. Neither of us smiled. There was a strange pull in the air between us.

"But it's nice to meet you," he said. And he nodded again and left the room. Emma and I exchanged a glance; for once we had no words.

☽

Mr. Palmer looked at me with big round eyes as I boarded the bus and gave me a nod and a slight smile. I returned the nod and looked for Su. And there she was, already on the bus. Already on the bus and sitting next to Ethan.

I took the seat in front of them. Su was smiling slyly. "You met Ethan, Tri?" she asked.

"In drama," I answered. I felt his eyes flick over my face. I turned away from them, strangely uncomfortable. And I had noticed, before I looked away, dark bruising on the side of his face that I didn't see before. There were also large scratchy marks running along his jaw line between his ear and his chin. *Was* he here because he had been in some kind of trouble? I listened to Su jabber—unusually talkative all of a sudden—as we rode home, and I felt his eyes on the back of my head, smelled the smell of him circling around me.

Winter was at the bus stop waiting in our old blue Subie—on time for once, a suspicious thing in itself. I lingered in my seat and let Su and Ethan leave before me. Mr. Palmer lifted his round eyes toward me as I walked past.

"Another day in history," I said, and he nodded.

"How's the driving coming?" he asked.

"Slow."

"Keep working on it. You'll get it."

"Thanks," I said and took a deep breath and left the bus. Su and Ethan were almost to the car. I suddenly wondered where he would sit. How would it be, being in such close quarters with him?

He slipped into the back with Su. I sank quickly into the front passenger seat and instantly felt Winter's eyes on me. What was it, I wondered—was I pale, was I sweating—what? Then I felt her look behind me at Ethan. A moment passed. Then the car moved forward and somehow, we made it home.

Ethan went directly to the guest cabin, and as I slid out of the car I heard Keats barking and growling in the entryway. I cut in front of Winter and beat her to the door.

"What is it, boy?" I asked, leaving the door wide open. "Show me. Come on—what's out here?"

Keats looked at me then lunged forward and began sniffing the ground around the car—on the side where Ethan got out. He started following the direction Ethan had walked, then stopped abruptly when he reached the side of the house. He lowered his head and began to growl. I walked over to him and cautiously stroked the top of his shoulders.

"It's okay, boy," I said. "It's okay." But I felt my own uneasiness growing. I looked toward the back of the house where Ethan had disappeared.

"He's just being protective," Winter said, suddenly standing beside me. "Ethan's a stranger here."

"He doesn't growl at the guests," I said.

I could feel Winter's discomfort. "I know," she said. "I think Ethan's energy is just—intense right now."

"Why?"

"Well, he's a long way from home, and he's a little upset."

"What's he upset about?"

Winter's face looked full to mine. "His father's dead and his mother doesn't want him," she said.

I couldn't reply. But the words were not lost on me.

The words stayed with me throughout the evening, from which Ethan was once again absent. Su helped Winter fix him a plate of food which Winter took out to him—much to Su's disappointment. "What do you think of him?" Su asked quickly, once Winter was out the back door.

"I don't know, Su," I said.

"Is it just because of Keats?" she asked.

"Is what because of Keats?"

"Do you not like him because Keats doesn't?"

"What makes you think I don't like him?"

"You're all prickly or something."

"I'm not."

"Yes—you are. I can *feel* it."

"You can *not*," I said. "And it's not that I don't like him. I don't know him. *We* don't know him—and neither does Winter."

"Well, I think he's nice."

"You think he's cute, Su—there's a difference."

"Well, you think he's cute too, don't you?"

"Su, any new boy in that school is going to be cute—even if he isn't."

"I just hope he likes it here," Su said. "I heard what Winter said—about his parents. He's like us, Tri—the same."

I knew I had to respond carefully. It was the same feeling I was fighting. "Similar circumstances don't make people the same," I said, trying to sound authoritative. "Different people are—different, even if they have a lot of things in common."

I could see how Su rolled her eyes.

Later, I took a bath and washed my hair. By the time I was done Su and Winter had gone to bed, and I sat in my pajamas in the dark of my and Su's room, untangling my long, wet mass of thick brown hair. I wanted badly to sit by the window and stare out at the nighttime woods, but I dared not and kept the curtains closed. Then I heard something—faint and distant, but there: a wolf's howl. I had always loved the sound, but tonight, somehow, it filled me with dread. I went to the window. In the faint light of the waning moon I saw a flurry of movement in front of Ethan's cabin. It seemed as if his door opened, he came out, and ran off into the woods. But I couldn't really tell. A moment later I heard the door to Winter's room open. I hardly breathed as I listened to her rush down the stairs. I stayed at the window, and then I saw her going out the back door: Winter in her light colored long-johns, running faster than I had ever seen anyone run—running into the woods, to wherever it was Ethan had gone.

☽

I waited that night, by the window, through the endless hours of darkness, waiting for one of them—or both of them—to return. I couldn't imagine what was happening, but what filled my thoughts the most was this: Ethan was insane. That's why he was here. That's why his mother didn't want him.

As hard as I tried not to, I drifted off. I dreamt a dream that I'd had before: I was in the woods, running and running and running through the brush and through the trees. Then I was on a high ridge that dropped abruptly down to a rushing stream. I smelled what was left of the fall: the cranberries, the rotting leaves, the dank dark smell of earth. Then the wind started blowing and snow started swirling through the night sky, swirling around me, and I was cold, so cold, and so far away from home.

I woke with a start. The house was dark and quiet. I looked out the window; there was nothing to see. I remembered my dream and realized I *was* cold; I found my clock and pushed the little light—it was 4 a.m. I looked at my bed. I could crawl into it and get warm, still get some sleep before my 7 a.m. alarm. And maybe they had already come back while I was dozing; maybe I had imagined the whole thing. Shivering, I succumbed and slipped beneath the heavy warm wool covers of my dear familiar bed. I thought maybe I would just lie there, get warm, and listen for any sounds. But before I knew it I fell asleep, and before I knew it my alarm was buzzing, and I opened my eyes.

Three

When Su and I were little, we'd hang around in the village park in the summer eating ice cream cones and waiting for our dad or Aunt Tabby to come and get us. Sometimes we would talk to the mountain climbers who would come there to pass the time while waiting for the weather to break so they could fly out to the mountains. We always told them our mother was a mountain climber, and we would ask if maybe they'd seen her. Long red hair. Tall—maybe, maybe she was tall. And her name was Julianne.

One spring there was a group of climbers from Argentina sprawled on a patch of scruffy grass which had emerged from the patches of snow and puddles of dirty water. Su and I left the swing where we were playing and walked over to them, the bottoms of our muddy jeans tucked into our tall rubber boots. The climbers—two men and one woman—didn't speak much English, but Su and I jabbered away at them anyway. And of course we asked them if they'd seen our mother.

Then one of the men said he knew a woman who had daughters with the names of mountains, like me and Su. But the woman's name was not Julianne. Still, Su and I jumped up and down and left the park—which we weren't supposed to do—to get our dad. We got into trouble instead—first with Aunt Tabby and then with our dad. By the time we made it back to the park, the climbers were gone. I waited every day for them to come back off the mountain, but they didn't make it and they never came down.

What Winter had said about Ethan—that his father was dead and his mother didn't want him—had made me start thinking about my own mother again. Where was she? Did she ever think of me and Su? Why hadn't she wanted us? As I lingered outside Winter's door that morning—the morning after I'd heard the wolf howl and thought I saw both Winter and Ethan running into the woods—I thought how strange it was, to have a mother out there somewhere—living and breathing and having breakfast and lunch and dinner—but have her be as inaccessible to me as my father who was no longer in the land of the living. They had both vanished: my father into nearby mountains after his small plane went down, my mother into the world. Gone without a trace.

And so here I was, waiting to wake up my strange stepmother, whose strange nephew was now part of my life. Wake her up and see if there was anything unusual about her, or her room, that could help me figure out where she and Ethan had been and what they had been doing. Because I knew, now that I was fully awake, that I hadn't imagined what I saw.

I knocked on the door. "Winter," I said. "It's time."

There was no response at first, then a muffled, "Okay."

I seized the opportunity to open the door. "What?" I asked as my eyes darted around the room.

"I said okay," Winter said, and she slowly pulled herself into a sitting position. Nothing seemed any different than any other morning. Then I saw one of her feet, sticking out from beneath the covers. The bottom was so dirty it looked as if it had been painted brown. "I'm coming," Winter said, and her foot disappeared as she swung her legs over the side of the bed.

"You should wash your feet," I said.

"What?"

I just raised my brows at her, turned and left the room. "Coffee's ready," I said over my shoulder.

As I was almost to the bottom of the stairs I heard Keats yelp suddenly, and Ethan appeared through the back door. I looked toward the open entryway door in time to see Keats retreat under the boot bench.

"Good morning," Ethan said. His dark hair curled down into his eyes. Like Winter, he looked extremely tired, but his face had a strange alertness—awareness—to it and I felt momentarily frozen in front of him. Like yesterday he dressed plainly in worn, faded clothes that looked almost too big for him: wrinkled khakis and a blue sweater with a hole in the shoulder. I wondered if he was poor. The clean musky smell of him drifted toward me.

"Su's made coffee," I said, and moved forward as quickly as I could.

In the kitchen, Su turned from the stove, looked beyond me and smiled. "Hi!" she said, beaming—or purring; it was like she was purring. "Coffee?" Her short black hair seemed glossier than usual, a straight silky sheen.

"We need to go soon," I said, glancing at the clock. But the first thing I did this morning was set it three additional minutes ahead. I just felt we'd need it.

"With milk?" Su said, ignoring me. "It's okay—Tri sets the clock ahead. We've got a few minutes."

That was enough. I sighed and grabbed my bag. "I'm going to start the car," I told Su. "You make sure Winter gets down those stairs."

"Don't worry," Su said. Then, as I left the room, I heard her say, "Hey—what happened to your face?"

I paused, pretending to adjust my bag.

"Nothing," I heard Ethan say. "Scratch."

"So all set, Tri?"

Winter. I whirled around and saw her standing at the bottom of the stairs. Her tired eyes lingered on me.

"Yeah," I said. "I'm just going to start the car. Su's got coffee."

"Oh. Good. Thank you. Tri—"

"Yes?"

"Are you all right?"

"Yes—why?"

"You look tired."

"Well," I said, "so do you." Then I hurried out the door.

I decided to sit in the back, near Su. I waited there until the three of them emerged from the house. Su looked annoyed but didn't say anything as she slipped in beside me. When Ethan got in I could smell him again.

He turned to say something, soft and low, to Winter, and I saw the side of his face. A bright red scratch, new since yesterday, crossed his cheek. Maybe he ran into a branch.

I remembered the wolf's howl that I'd heard, just shortly before I saw Ethan run off. Normally that would have been something I would have told Winter about right away. Though we weren't far from wolf country, it was rare that they wandered in so close to town.

"I heard a wolf last night," I said, leaning forward just a little to be sure Winter could hear me. Both she and Ethan whipped around and looked at me. I saw in that flash of an instant a certain similarity in their features; they were definitely related. But I also saw that at that moment no one was watching the road. "Winter," I said. "Watch the road."

"Oh! Sorry, Tri. You're right." And she swerved away from the ditch.

Ethan continued to look at me, and there was something on his face, as if he wanted to ask me something but the words wouldn't come. Then his eyes blinked, and he turned back around. Su and I exchanged a glance.

"What time did you hear it?" Su asked.

"I don't know. Midnight maybe."

"Why were you still awake?"

"My hair was wet."

"Oh." And no one mentioned it again.

☽

School drug on like never before, or maybe it just seemed that way. I was tired and worried—about what exactly, I didn't know. And everybody was asking me about Ethan; I was quickly becoming tired of being everybody's new best friend. And my real best friend— Emma—was the worst; she wanted to know every detail of every moment I saw him and every nuance of every word he spoke. And then finally we had biology and Jack—a diversion—was in that class. But then, I realized, so was Ethan. He sat toward the back while we were in the front, so I couldn't see him. But I felt him, his presence, and I kept getting little shivery feelings on the back of my neck, as if he was breathing on me from all the way across the length of the room. Then, at the end of lunch break, he said to me, "You don't like it that I'm here."

I was by myself at a table by the front windows. I hadn't heard him—hadn't seen him—slip onto the bench across from me. I was too startled to respond.

"It's okay," he said softly. "I understand. And I'm sorry about it. My mother didn't give me a choice."

I met his dark eyes. "We don't know you," I said.

"No." For a moment we just looked at each other. I suddenly felt like I was out of air.

"You're different," I managed to say. But I could see how those words brought a slight smile to the corner of his mouth.

"So are you," he said, rising from the table and leaning a little toward me, his voice barely above a whisper and sending shivers down my spine. "Trileka Tyler."

I didn't see him much the rest of the day, but I kept imagining I could smell him in the hall, smell him in the different classrooms I entered, as if part of him lingered in the air he passed through.

☽

Tabby and Sydney showed up that night for dinner. Winter had actually cooked; I smelled it the second I walked in the door—some kind of a roast—so I knew something special was going on. Winter usually didn't cook meals that took hours to prepare. She didn't think far enough ahead for that. It was a caribou roast, and I sat at the table fingering through my homework until Tabby and Sydney came in the front door and we sat down to eat.

Winter lingered at the stove while we waited for her to set the roast on the table. I heard Keats out in the entryway—first growling, then barking, then making a sound that was something between a growl and a whine. The back door opened and he yelped and fell silent. I held my breath, and Ethan entered the house.

"Hey, mate," Sydney said, standing and reaching out his hand when Ethan crossed into the kitchen. "I'm Sydney, this is Tabby, and we're glad to meet you."

Ethan shook Sydney's hand and bowed his head at Tabby, who tipped her own head forward slightly in return. I watched curiously, suspiciously; where does one learn such a gesture? Ethan then took a seat next to Su, who was sitting next to me, across from Tabby and Sydney. Winter placed the roast in the center of the table and took her place at the head. "May I?" Sydney asked her, raising the carving knife. Winter nodded and Sydney carved the meat and placed thick slabs on each plate. Then I noticed a strange tension in the air and that Su, Tabby, Winter, and Ethan were all staring at their plates. I looked at mine but could see nothing wrong—just a piece of meat, waiting for gravy and vegetables. I looked at Sydney, who was suddenly very still. His eyes met mine for the quickest of moments, then he said: "Well, let's dig in, shall we, and pass the veges around?" But I was the only one who took any vegetables at that moment. The others—everyone except me and Sydney—were devouring their caribou like they hadn't eaten in a week.

"Nothing like a good old caribou roast," Sydney said, putting some mashed potatoes on his plate and passing them across to me. I took some then elbowed Su—hard. Her face turned toward mine. She was chewing so fast juice from the meat was leaking down the corner of her mouth. And she looked oddly angry—angry at being disturbed.

What's wrong with you? I mouthed. What was wrong with everybody?

"Good meat," Su whispered.

"It's caribou, Su, it's been in the freezer a long time and it's not that good," I said, loudly and openly and not without a good deal of irritation. "No offense, Winter—I'm sure it tastes fine." Then whatever had fallen over the table lifted, and the vegetables and potatoes went around and there was talking and laughing just like any other time with Sydney and Tabby over—except for the quiet presence of the dark-haired boy sitting next to my suddenly starving sister.

After dinner I washed up while everyone else went into the living room. Sydney stayed behind to give me a hand.

"What's with Keatsie boy?" he asked, bringing me some more dishes from the table. Scrapings from the plates lay unnoticed in Keats' dish.

I shrugged and looked through the passageway toward the living room. "I don't think he likes Ethan," I said quietly.

"Oh," Sydney said. "Dark lad, isn't he? Kind of mysterious."

I breathed a sigh of relief. "You mean I'm not the only one who thinks so?"

"Oh, no Tri—Tab and I have been wondering how it's been out here."

"I heard a wolf last night," I said, not sure why I was bringing that up.

Sydney didn't say anything and grabbed a towel to start drying dishes.

"Wolves don't come around here very often," I added.

"But they do, sometimes, pass through, you know?" Sydney said, and we finished the dishes in silence.

Later that night, before we went to bed, Winter'd said, "Temperature's going to drop," and it did; I woke up to morning darkness and the feeling of the increased cold on the end of my nose. I wondered how I'd slept all night. I hadn't intended on sleeping at all, but I'd gotten cold sitting in my chair by the window and crawled into bed to warm up for a while. But "for a while" turned into the rest of the night, and now I didn't know what happened other than it had grown substantially colder. I got up, carefully lifted a corner of the curtain, and tried to see. It looked sleepy and quiet out—a hint of light was starting to emerge from the edges of the sky. Maybe I didn't miss anything. Maybe there was nothing to miss. It was Saturday, so I went back to bed and slid beneath the warm covers. I didn't wake up again for several more hours, and when I did, I could hear that Dangerous Dan—our crazy neighbor—was down in the entryway talking with Winter. I slipped out of bed and poked my head out the door.

"I heard it, too," he was saying. "Or maybe I should say them— there was definitely more than one at one point."

"They're just wolves," Winter said.

"Easy to say at the moment," Dan said. "Just wolves. I tracked the one all the way over here to your property—that doesn't bother you at all?"

"No, not really."

"Well, they're not what the wolf lovers make them out to be, you know. They don't sit around writing wolf poetry and singing folk songs. If you had a dog yard maybe you'd understand. I've heard the stories, and if I see 'em, I'm killing 'em."

I stood listening in the hallway above the stairs, picturing Dan in my mind: thin black hair parted straight down the middle and pulled back into a ponytail; bulging green eyes behind wire framed glasses, which always tended to slip down his beak-like nose; huge army-surplus mukluks on his feet—even this time of year—which made him look as if he was standing in a block of olive green cement. And the ever-present rifle in his arms. That's why we called him Dangerous Dan.

Winter was still standing in the entryway after Dan left and I came down the stairs. I could tell she was lost in thought, staring at the door with Keats at her side; I brushed past her and went to the kitchen to make coffee. A moment later she was in the kitchen, appearing so silently and suddenly that I nearly dropped the glass carafe of the electric coffee pot we "borrowed" from one of the guest cabins when it was empty. She looked past me out the window above the sink. Then just as suddenly she left, returning back up the stairs.

A movement out the window on the side wall caught my eye; Dangerous Dan was still outside, snooping around. I clicked on the coffee pot, slipped on my boots and coat in the entry and went outside,

Keats following.

The air was sharp and cold, and a steely gray sky hinted at snow. I followed Dan's tracks around to the side of the house and caught him bending over and looking at some tracks near the guest cabin where Ethan slept.

"Can I help you?" I asked. My dad never had much patience with Dan and his weird antics, and I didn't, either.

"I'm just looking, Tri, just looking. You've had a wolf on your property."

"I think you've already talked to Winter about that. And I don't think she's too worried."

He straightened, shook his head and clucked his tongue. "As I said, wolves don't sit around—"

"Writing wolf poetry and singing folk songs."

"They're killers, Tri. Fierce carnivores. They'd eat your dog if they had half a chance."

"They won't get a chance," I said. "That's what houses are for."

"Yeah, well, I've got more than one dog, and I can't bring the whole team in to keep them safe."

"I'm sure you'll figure something out."

"Oh—damn right I will. We're not the superior animals we are for nothing."

"Good," I said. "Then you should probably go and make sure they're safe."

He shot me a sullen glance. "All right, Miss Trileka. Keep me posted—let me know if you see or hear anything."

"All right," I said.

And finally he walked away.

Our conversation had taken place just outside Ethan's cabin. I looked at it awkwardly, wondering what he'd heard or if we'd woken him up. The big front window was there, so close to where I was. I took a tentative step forward and tried to see inside. All I could see was that it looked like an incredible mess. Then Keats growled and retreated.

"Hello, Trileka."

I froze. He appeared from around the corner of the guest cabin, his eyes dark, his face pale, and his black glossy hair falling forward. I fumbled for words, but he knelt down near where Dan had stood and looked at the boot tracks in the snow, seeming to ignore the wolf tracks, which looked equally fresh.

"Big feet for not so big a man," he said.

I noticed Ethan's wrists and his hands sticking out from the sleeves of his jacket. His wrists were thin, and his fingers were long and nicely shaped; his skin was pale and luminous in the morning cold. "I think he just wears big boots," I said, tearing my eyes away. "I think he thinks that's the Alaskan way."

Ethan continued to look at the ground. He didn't mention the wolf tracks, but he seemed to be taking in the entire area.

"I've got some coffee going," I said. "You could come inside, if you like."

His eyes narrowed as he looked up at me. "Okay," he said. "Thank you." And he followed me back to the front of the house. Keats was near the door, but he waited until Ethan stepped through it before I could coax him back into the entryway.

In the kitchen, I poured coffee and turned around to hand Ethan a cup, but suddenly he wasn't there. Then I heard a growl. Ethan was on his hands and knees, near the entry doorway, having a stare-down with Keats. I held my breath as Ethan reached out a hand toward the unhappy dog. To my surprise, though, Keats came a little closer, first smelled then tentatively licked Ethan's outstretched fingers. But Keats quickly pulled back and withdrew to the entryway. Ethan rose, turned and saw me watching.

I said nothing, but our eyes met for a strange moment. I felt as if he felt my continued wariness and my concern—and was letting me know he felt it. But the moment passed, like a curtain closing. I handed him his coffee, goose bumps rising on my arm as he accepted the mug and we almost touched.

"Thank you," he said quietly.

I went over to the table and put it between us, sitting on one side with him on the other. I pushed the can of evaporated milk and the jar of sugar toward him. He put some of each into his coffee, glancing cautiously at me as if we were playing chess and he was waiting for me to make a move. I was careful, though, not to let my eyes lock onto his again.

"What do you do out there?" I asked.

His eyes flashed. "In your guest house?" he asked.

"Yes."

"Read. Sleep. Look out the window and think."

"What do you read?"

"Sherlock Holmes."

For some reason that surprised me. It seemed, well, interesting and normal at the same time. "What else?"

"Robert Louis Stevenson."

I suppressed a smile. "*Treasure Island.*"

He nodded. "*Kidnapped.* That's probably my favorite." He lifted his mug a little, holding it with both hands, and seemed to sniff his coffee before taking some quick drinks. It grew quiet again. I was becoming aware of the thudding of my heart—as if I could literally hear it—when he said, "What do you like to read, Trileka Tyler?" His eyes lifted in my direction.

I felt suddenly flustered. I liked the way he said my name; I liked the way he seemed to like to say it. "Emily Bronte," I managed. "And Charlotte Bronte, Shakespeare. . . Charles Dickens." Dead writers, times long passed. Emma once asked me, *Don't you read anybody who's still alive?*

"I like Shakespeare," Ethan said. Then he cocked his head to one side, as if he was listening to something I couldn't hear, and said, "Your sister's awake." In the next instant I heard Su's feet flop down on the floor above us. A minute later the sound of the toilet flushing washed through the house, and Su came bounding down the stairs. She paused on the threshold to the kitchen, her pleasure at seeing Ethan evident.

"Su, it's cold. You'll get cold," I said. Her t-shirt seemed too thin and her boxers seemed too short. She ignored me and gave Ethan a strange smile. His face twitched. Su slunk over to the refrigerator, swung open the door and grabbed a gallon of milk. She opened it, put it to her lips and tipped her head back, drinking deeply.

"I'm thirsty," she said, out of breath and with her voice strangely husky. She wiped her mouth with her arm and put the milk back inside the fridge. I looked at her, dumbfounded. Then I realized Ethan was watching me watch Su, who poured herself some coffee and straddled a chair next to him. I let my eyes meet his. "It's going to snow today," he said. Then, to Su's great disappointment, he thanked me for the coffee, rose from the table, and left.

Four

It was a quiet day. Something had settled on the house along with the new blanket of snow—as Ethan had predicted—that was falling in tight, small flakes. Winter was pale and kept looking out the window as she went from one craft project to another: a pair of mittens she was knitting for Su, a watercolor of the Alaska Range she was painting for one of the guest cabins, and a bag of dog hair she was preparing to spin into yarn, which she would later dye with Kool-Aid. Ethan appeared once or twice and spoke quietly with Winter. Su seemed normal—wandering around with her iPod and her earbuds in, trying on outfits for school. I sat at the kitchen table with my books open, unable to concentrate. Something just didn't feel right. I looked at Winter, across the table from me, pulling and twisting dog hair. Suddenly she stopped, her eyes went strangely bright, and she tipped her head slightly first this way then that, like a bird in a tree, listening. Then some sort of shadow crossed her face at the same time Keats' low growl came from the entryway. I opened my mouth to ask, but she put her fingers to her lips and slid silently out of her chair. She cautiously peered out the window by the sink, then the big window on the side wall, angling herself to see back toward the guest cabin.

"Wolves," she said, whispering.

Though she motioned for me to stay still, I quietly moved over to the window and looked.

And there were wolves. Wolves, not wolf. Wolves. I counted three—four, five, and then six. Six wolves. A gray and white one. One with white, gray and brown markings. One that was mostly black, one that was mostly gray, one that was mostly white and brown, and then one that seemed to be all black—all black, and the largest of the group. A pack. They seemed interested in the tracks around the guest cabin—the wolf tracks, Dan's tracks, my tracks, Ethan's.

"Tri, get the shotgun and fire out the back door."

"What?"

"We need to scare them away."

"Why?"

"Because we do. I need you to do it. I need to—I need to watch Keats."

I looked questioningly at Winter. She was never afraid of anything. Bears, moose—anything. Su and I were sure she was going to get stomped or charged someday. Compared to some of the bears we've had in our yard, these wolves didn't seem as bad. But there was something about the whole pack thing. Then why was she sending me out there?

Su appeared in the kitchen threshold. Winter said flatly: "Su, go upstairs."

"What?" Su pulled down her earbuds.

"Go upstairs, Su. Now. Now!"

Su and I looked at each other, and Su hurried back the way she came. Before Winter had a chance to ask me again, I pulled my dad's shotgun down from its place high on the kitchen wall and headed for the back door. Winter wouldn't have asked me if it hadn't been important—that much I knew. I was suddenly afraid she was worried about Su, though I couldn't understand why. I pumped a shell into the chamber, clicked off the safety and swung open the back door.

"Out!" I yelled. "Get out of here!" I pointed the barrel upwards and fired. The gun kicked back against my shoulder, and a loud explosion filled the air. The wolves froze and looked at me. Nothing happened. I pumped another shell, lifted the gun and fired again. This time they moved, though I could sense a reluctance in their leaving as they slunk away.

"Get Ethan," Winter now said. She was pressed against the wall by the entryway, staying out of view of the back door.

Without questioning I ran the short distance to the guest cabin and pounded on the door. "Ethan!" I said. "Ethan!" There was no answer. I threw open the door.

The place was noticeably cleaner; his clothes were heaped into a pile on top of his back-pack, and the covers that had been strewn all over the couch were neatly folded. The floor was swept. But where was he?

Then I saw him, in a far corner, peering at me through the dimness of the unlit room.

"Ethan," I said. "Winter wants you in the house. There are some wolves—" I looked at him. He seemed to be shaking. "What's wrong?"

He shook his head and pulled himself from the corner. We rushed out the door. His eyes moved wildly at the array of tracks as we hurried across the small distance to the back door. The moment we were inside Winter pulled the blind down on the door's window and bolted the door shut. "Thank you, Tri," she said. I returned the gun to its post on the kitchen wall then went toward the stairs, glancing briefly at Ethan and Winter, who were talking quietly together in the little hallway by the back door, before running up to Su.

I opened the door to our room. "Su?" At first the only thing I noticed was that the window was open, and a cold snowy wind was whipping the curtains around. Momentarily panicked, I ran to the window and stuck my head out, expecting to see Su sprawled on the ground below. But there was nothing, and the snow there was undisturbed. Then I realized Su was sitting in the middle of her bed, completely covered by a quilt. I approached her slowly and touched her gently; she seemed to be trembling. "Su?" I said. "Su, are you okay?"

"What did they want?" she said, her voice high and tight.

"Who? What did who want?"

"The wolves! What did they want?"

I felt my brow furrow and a tension building there, between my eyes. "The wolves didn't want anything, Su, they were just there. What are you talking about?"

The form under the quilt began to move, then, and after a moment Su's face emerged, pale and stressed looking. "They wanted something, Tri. I know they did!"

"Su, how could you know something like that? They're wild animals, they're curious, just like the—"

"No, Tri, no. They wanted something. I could feel it. I could *feel* them wanting something!"

"How could you—"

Then Winter appeared in the doorway to our room. "What's wrong?"

"Su thinks the wolves wanted something," I said.

"They did! Winter, I felt them!"

A strange look passed over Winter's face, and she came over to the bed and sat next to Su. "Su, it's all right, the wolves are gone. Tri scared them away."

Su looked at me. "You did?"

I nodded.

"But they're not gone," she said.

I looked out the window. "Yes, they are."

"No, they're not!"

And as if to have the final say, at that moment a single howl rose from the woods around our house—joined soon by another, and another, and another still. Su nodded her head, glaring angrily at me as if it were my fault. Winter put an arm around her and held her close. "We're safe here, Su, no matter what they want," Winter said. "Your dad built a good house—a good safe house. Tri?"

I looked at her.

"Will you go check on Ethan? I'll stay here with Su."

I nodded, not sure why Ethan needed checking on. I went back downstairs. "Ethan?" Again he seemed to be nowhere, and again I found him, after a small search, standing pressed into a dim corner of the living room. His dark eyes looked at me.

I suddenly flashed on one of my favorite books—*Wuthering Heights* by Emily Bronte. An image of Heathcliff in a dark corner, looking out at Katherine. I stopped myself and gritted my teeth. "Don't they have wolves in Canada?" I asked, knowing full well they did. "Let me know if you need anything," I said and turned back toward the kitchen. But then I heard, before I was quite out of the living room: "Yes."

I looked behind me. Ethan had come out of the corner and stood looking at me, hands in the pockets of his baggy brown pants.

"What?"

"I said yes. There are wolves in Canada. Lots of wolves."

"Oh," I said. "Good."

"I'm not scared of the wolves, Tri. Trileka."

"Okay." I waited for him to say something more. But he didn't— he just looked at me until I had to turn away.

I spent the rest of the afternoon alone in the kitchen with Keats. Su and Winter remained upstairs, and Ethan remained in the living room. Soon the daylight began to fade, and I realized that not only had I forgotten to feed the woodstove, but I would likely need to haul more wood into the house for the night. I walked tentatively to the living room. To my surprise there was Ethan, stoking a blazing fire.

"Thanks," I said. "I forgot."

He nodded and jimmied a log into place and closed the door. The fire was fed through a side door; the front of the stove was made of cast iron and glass, giving a view of the flickering flames within. "It's getting dark," he said.

I looked at the few pieces of wood left by the stove. "I need to bring in some wood."

He looked across the room at me. "Is that necessary?"

"Well, yes, if we want to stay warm tonight."

He paused a moment, then bowed his head as if conceding something. "All right," he said. "I'll go out there with you."

"It's okay. I've been bringing in the wood since I was six years old." He was about to say something, then I added, "Wolves don't hurt people. Of course there have been a few exceptions; there are always a few exceptions. But those stories are rare."

Something flickered across his face. I did know about wolves, their habits and how they fit into history: Wolves emerged somewhere in the middle of the Ice Age. They probably evolved from other dog-like creatures, as did dogs and foxes. My father had a wide collection of books about wolves, which we still kept on a shelf in the living room. I often found myself drawn to them, though there was one I would not touch. An old book. *The Book of Were-Wolves: Being an Account of a Terrible Superstition* by Sabine Baring-Gould. I could remember looking at it once. And once was enough. "I'm going to get the wood now," I said quickly, turning and leaving the room. "You don't have to help."

"I would like to," he said.

I looked into the dim-dark room, looked at him. His face was open as he stared at me, waiting for an answer, his eyes questioning.

"Okay."

In the entryway I pulled a pair of extra mittens from the drying basket and handed them to Ethan. He said a quiet thank you and followed me outside. The snow continued to fall, and I noticed the delicate white flakes landing in his thick dark hair. I began to fill my arms; Ethan did the same. We both reached for the same piece of wood and our faces came close. The smell of his skin was powerful in my nose, and I heard him take several short, sharp breaths as if he, too, was smelling me. Then our eyes met and I felt a jolt in my stomach. Strange sensations rippled through me. He was so close. His eyes were so dark and so full of something—something I seemed to know. I suddenly wanted to touch him so badly even though I had no idea why I would want to do that.

There was a slight shake of his head. "I shouldn't be here," he said, his voice a whisper. "Though I'm not sorry I met you."

My heart thumped. "Why shouldn't you be here?" Somehow, I could feel the warmth of his skin and I stared longingly at the side of his face, his lips—

"But maybe I can help you, Trileka."

I didn't know what he meant. My thoughts felt thick and slow, and something kept pulling me toward him, as if we were two magnets on the verge of slamming into each other.

Then suddenly he moved his head back and up, and the moment was broken. He looked quickly from side to side, his eyes darting and his face alert.

"What is it?" I asked. The extra inches between us now seemed to free me from whatever was tugging at me, and I felt my head clear though a weak-feeling sensation lingered in my knees.

"I thought I heard something," he said. There was concern on his face.

I thought for a moment that maybe he'd heard my heart. Or the blood in my veins. But I knew what he was thinking: wolves. He began grabbing wood again, and I did the same, my eyes glimpsing at the thick trees surrounding our house. We worked in silence, going back and forth a number of times, piling the wood in the living room until it seemed we had more than enough. I went back outside for one last load and froze. Ethan was by the woodshed, arms full, standing as still as a statue. And not twenty feet from him was a wolf, the big black one, and from where I stood it looked as if they were staring at each other.

My mind raced. Then I grabbed a shovel from beside the doorway and moved cautiously forward, heart pounding, until I stood near Ethan.

"I have to go inside," he whispered. I could see his face from the corner of my eye; he seemed to be twitching, and his breathing sounded ragged and unsteady.

"Okay," I whispered back. The wolf looked at me and I looked at him and our eyes met. I felt strangely unafraid, but I also felt that I was somehow—in his way. Or something.

"You come, too," Ethan whispered.

I nodded, and in unison we began backing away from the wolf and toward the house. As the wolf turned silently and loped unhurriedly back into the trees, Winter burst out of the doorway and grabbed Ethan and pulled him, wood falling from his arms, back inside. I took a quick look at the woods around the house and followed. As I came through the entryway Ethan was tilted face-first into a corner by the back door and Winter was whispering to him fiercely. Su was standing on the stairs, crying.

"Is he all right?" I asked. Ethan was visibly shaking. *Drugs*, I thought; *maybe he's on drugs.*

"He's fine," Winter said. "He's just having a—an episode."

"Like a seizure?"

"Yes—yes. Like a seizure. Tri—see to your sister, please."

I looked at Su. "Su, stop crying," I said. "You are not afraid of wolves!"

"But Tri—"

"Su, you're acting crazy! Now come down and be normal!" I took a deep breath. "There's a good fire going," I added, trying to sound less stern. "It will cheer you up. Maybe we should all go in the living room." I looked at Ethan and Winter. "Come on, Su."

Reluctantly Su made her way down, and I walked with her into the living room where the fire still burned bright and cheerful. I guided her to a chair and she sank down into it, looking fearfully at the windows. I closed the curtains to placate her and went to the kitchen and made a pot of hot cocoa. I carried this and a cluster of mugs back into the living room, where Winter and Ethan now sat with Su. I felt Ethan watching me as I silently filled cups and passed them around; he was terribly pale and seemed to be concentrating on steadying himself, his hands shaking as he tried to lift a mug. "I'm going to make dinner now," I announced, and carried away the empty pot.

I made burritos, deliberately leaving out meat. There'd been enough meat on the table last night. I carried the burritos on plates into the living room, placed the plates on the homemade coffee table and sat down. No one seemed interested in the food. Outside somewhere, beyond the walls, a wolf howled. Inside, the silence grew.

Five

The wolves left that night, and for the next few days they stayed away, but a strange tension had settled on the house. During this time Ethan helped me bring in the wood. He was silent, but he kept looking at me, and I felt like he wanted to say something. I had also noticed, though, in the past several days, that he watched Su almost constantly. I felt an unfamiliar squeezing on my heart and wondered at it.

We didn't get any more snow, and the temperature dropped well below freezing and it seemed it would stay there. Old Man Winter was knocking on the door now, as my father used to say. At night as I sat alone in my and Su's room, I would place my hand on the window and feel the cold on the other side of the glass, pressing up against it.

I was sitting like this one night when I watched Ethan return to the guest cabin, his movements illuminated by an echo of light from the house. He reached the door and stopped, turning and looking up at the window of my unlit room, and I was too slow to move. Through the dark and the distance his eyes found mine. We stared at each other. I moved my hand in a small wave. Then a smile spread slowly across his face—a quiet smile but a real smile, his whole face responding to the gentle upward turn of his lips as dimples winked in his cheeks and just below his bright dark eyes. It lasted only a second before he turned and went inside the guest cabin, but the smile replayed in my thoughts as I sat frozen by the window, staring at the now empty spot where he had stood.

That night I dreamt I was in the woods again, running, only this time I was looking for Su. It was all shadows, and I couldn't see and I heard wolves in the woods, wolves. Around a tree and there was Ethan. His eyes found mine and I tried to speak, tried to tell him about Su. But all I could do was look at him. "Trileka Tyler," he whispered, and as our faces drew closer I knew I was going to kiss him—but something was happening to Su, I didn't know where she was and something was wrong—

I woke up with a start. The room was dark and cold, but relief flooded through me. It was just a dream. But as I looked at Su's bed I felt my heart sink in my chest: it was empty—Su wasn't there.

I rushed to the window and looked out at the moonless night, the snow-covered ground ghostly and barely visible. Then I saw movement, also ghostly white, near Ethan's guest cabin. My eyes strained. Su's white nightgown. And she wasn't alone. A glimpse of a pale face. She was with Ethan. They were close—was he holding her? My hand went to my open mouth, and I felt a rush of adrenaline as well as a feeling I didn't recognize—a strangling feeling, one that wrapped itself tightly around me and made me want to scream.

I heard the back door open, and I hurriedly returned to bed. Su entered the room and slipped under her covers. I could smell the night on her—the fresh cold air. And I smelled—or thought I could smell—*him*.

I lay with a thundering heart in my chest until my alarm shrieked through the silence.

That morning, I tried to act normal as we rushed to get ready for school, but I was shaking inside and out. Winter looked at me quizzically; she always seemed to sense when something was wrong. But she didn't ask, and I was grateful for that, as I didn't know yet what to do. Should I just tell Winter, or should I ask Su? I didn't want to ask Su. I didn't want to know. But know what? She was my little sister. My little sister.

I thought about telling Emma, but she wasn't outside when the bus came, and later when I saw her down the hall she was talking to Chris Evans. I stopped. They were standing fairly close. Then she saw me and turned away from him abruptly, making her way over to me.

"What was that about?" I asked her.

"Nothing," she said. "He's just a jerk."

"Why do you say that? What did he say?"

She shook her head. "Really, Tri—nothing. In fact, I can't even remember!"

But I didn't believe her. The moment hung over us and followed us through the day, like a dark cloud.

Later, after school, I told Su to grab her skates, and we would go ice skating. I had to do something. Something familiar, familiar and fun. And normal.

"What about Ethan?" she asked as we went to a corner of the woodshed where our winter sports things were stored. The skates hung from nails in the wall.

"What about him? All he does is hole up in the guest cabin."

"What are you grumpy about?"

"I'm not grumpy."

"Yes, you are!"

"I am not."

"Yes, you are! I can *feel* it—"

"I saw you!" I snapped, anger as sudden as a flash flood washing through me. "Outside last night. With Ethan."

"*What?*"

"You heard me. I saw you."

"Saw me what?"

"Saw you outside with Ethan!"

"When?"

"Last night!"

"Like last night when?"

"Like in the middle of the night!"

"Like after we went to bed?"

I nodded. The rush of anger I'd felt was subsiding, and I could see the confusion on her face.

"I don't know what you're talking about," she said.

"You don't?"

"No! Are you freaking out or something?"

"Su, I saw you—you were outside, and you weren't in your bed. I checked. Then I watched you come back in. Don't you remember?"

She shook her head, and I saw her face beginning to pale. "Maybe you were dreaming?"

"I don't think so," I said.

"Maybe it wasn't me?"

"No, it was you."

"Well, you must have been dreaming," she said.

I didn't say anything more. It didn't seem like Su was lying, but I knew what I'd seen. Could she have been sleepwalking? Could I have been dreaming?

Or had Su simply gotten *better* at lying?

As we walked past the house, our skates in hand, Winter appeared in the doorway. "I'll meet you down there," she said.

"You don't have to," I said.

But she disappeared back inside, and I knew she was thinking about the wolves.

We walked down the hill and out onto the main road, Keats loping along beside us. After about a half mile we left the roadway and walked down a ridge to a small oval lake, which in its newly-frozen state looked like a milky jewel or a cloudy mirror. Su was unusually quiet. I wondered what that meant.

On the ice we went our separate ways. "Don't go too far from the shore," I called after her. I'd evaluated the ice beneath me and determined that it likely was frozen solidly all the way across. Still, it was our first time out.

Then Keats looked up and I saw something moving on the far side of the lake—fast, graceful. Another skater. Then a second one, and I recognized Winter. So the first one was Ethan. They were both fast and flawless, and Winter headed toward me and Su while Ethan lingered near the far shore. They must have cut straight through the woods, I determined, in order to catch up to me and Su.

Winter waved to me and joined Su; I continued in the opposite direction, concentrating on the sleek feel of the ice beneath my skates, Keats coming along beside me, his paws slipping on the smooth surface. I could see Ethan skating in a small cove; he skated backwards, forwards, backwards again, his movements fluid and graceful. Then he began skating toward me, and I braced for an encounter.

He glided up to me then came abruptly to a halt. The brisk air brought color to his cheeks and to the tip of his nose; he was hatless, and his curls looped and flipped haphazardly around his face. As he looked at me his eyes were steady but questioning. What could he see, there on my face?

I tried to think of something to say but nothing came. I wondered if I should just ask him about what I'd seen the night before. I reached out and touched poor unhappy Keats, who stood glumly beside me.

Then some kind of curtain parted between us and everything else seemed to fall away as we looked at each other. With an easy stride he closed the distance between us, and Keats slipped a little as he reacted to the movement; I started to lose balance. But as my feet were moving out from under me Ethan came alongside me and reached out his hand. I grabbed hold and he pulled me up, and I felt myself moving toward him as if in a dream.

Then something out on the ice caught my eye. It was Su, cutting straight across the middle of the lake, heading toward us.

"Su!" I shouted, and turned on my skates, releasing Ethan. "Don't!" Then it was like in a nightmare: Su began losing her balance, and I could see it was because the ice was shattering beneath her. I began lunging forward but Ethan pulled me backwards and let me go so that I slid toward the shore. "Stay here," he said, and he rushed forward while I crashed into snow and ground. I saw Su disappear and Ethan skate right into the hole in the ice that she had made. They emerged before I could even get back on my feet, and Ethan shoved Su up onto the ice and pushed her so she slid on her belly away from the jagged break in the surface. She continued to crawl forward, heading for the nearest shore, and behind her Ethan pulled himself out of the water and did likewise. By now Winter was nearby and waited on the thicker ice. I found my feet again and hurried to meet her. By the time I reached Winter, Su was starting to pull herself up.

"Did you see that?" Su asked. "Did you see Ethan?"

"I told you to stay near shore!" I said. I felt a knot of anger and fear in my chest. "I told you! You could have died!"

"Tri—" Winter began.

"She could have died!" I snapped. I turned back to Su. "Come on— we need to get you home before you get hypothermia!"

"I'm not cold, Tri."

"Of course you are!"

"No, I'm not! Really, I'm okay! Quit yelling at me already!"

I looked at her and Ethan, both vertical now and wet and dripping. But not shivering. I looked at Winter. She said, softly, "They're fine, Tri, but we'll hurry home."

I was shaking. I felt like all three of them were looking at me. So I skated away, rushing to where I'd stashed my boots by the shore, and even Keats didn't bother to try to follow me.

When I got home, I put on a pot of stew for supper and went upstairs to wash my hair. I heard the others return and heard Su run upstairs to our room to change then run back down again. I waited in the bathroom as long as I could, just wanting to be alone, then I went back downstairs to check on the stew. The house was quiet and almost dark. As I entered the kitchen I saw Su there, sitting in darkness at the table—eating already. I felt my stomach tighten.

"Su—it's not done yet," I said, turning on a light.

She looked at me, her mouth full and moving. After she swallowed she said, "You ruined the meat, Tri. There's nothing to it anymore. The flavor's all washed out."

I looked at her. All I could think of to say was, "You used to like stew."

"Well," she said, "now I don't." She shoved her bowl toward the center of the table, got up and left the kitchen. I walked over to the stew pot, still boiling away but with the lid haphazardly left on the stovetop near the burner. I found the stirring spoon, also on the stovetop, and dipped it into the stew. The meat was all gone—every last piece. All that remained were lonely vegetables floating in a watery broth.

What was happening to her?

I felt someone enter the room. Ethan. I knew, somehow, that it was him. I turned and we looked across the room at each other. His eyes searched my face then shifted to the spoon in my hand. "Su ate the meat," I said. "In the stew."

I saw a tinge of scarlet flood his cheeks and he looked away. "I'm sorry you got upset," he said. He was talking about earlier, on the ice.

"Su doesn't always think," I responded, aware of my betrayal. But I knew what Su had been doing. She'd seen that Ethan was with me. That's why she was rushing across the ice. "Anyway, thank you for saving her." I kept my voice curt. The ice-skating incident and the stew had distracted me, but I had not for a minute forgotten what it seemed I had seen.

"She would have been all right," he said. I could feel his eyes searching my face; he had noticed my tone.

"I'm not so sure about that."

"You worry about her a lot."

"Someone has to." I shot him a glance. Our eyes connected for a brief second then I looked away.

"I can help you, Tri," he said, so very quietly I could barely hear him.

Our eyes met again. His hair was still wet and dripping. This was the second time he'd said he could help me. Why did he think I needed help?

But I couldn't bring myself to ask and tore my eyes from his. He turned and left the room. I stared at Su's empty bowl. Did Ethan know something I didn't?

Six

For the next few days, the house stayed quiet, the temperature stayed cold, and the wolves continued to stay away. And—as far as I could tell—Su stayed in her bed at night, though I was nearly delirious from sleep deprivation. Thursday came—the day before Halloween—and Su and I had not worked on our costumes yet— something we should have already been doing.

Su was sullen. She had been sullen since our talk in the woodshed once the thrill of Ethan saving her had worn off. "I'm not sure I want to go," she said.

"Su—we always go." Even though we now felt too old to trick-or-treat, Su and I would meet up with Emma and Jack down in the village and run through the cold streets. It was something to do. When we were done we'd go to a local restaurant for hot chocolate and we'd laugh and talk as we thawed out in the warm log front room of the Altitude. We always looked forward to it.

"I'll bet Ethan won't go," Su now said.

"Ethan can do what he wants—why do you care?" The words came out more sharply than I'd intended. It wasn't lost on me that Su's face would light up whenever he walked into a room. And he still watched her, slyly, out of the corner of his eye. I was consumed with wondering what was going on with them, and as each day went by I failed to tell anyone about what I thought I had seen. "Well," I said, trying a softer tone, "I'm going to go. You can do what you want."

"All right," Su said. "I'll go. But I'll need help with my costume."

"Sure," I said. "Help" usually meant Su would come up with the idea and I would do all the work. We were in the living room, and I stood and began walking to the doorway to find the cardboard box of material. "What are you thinking of being?"

"A wolf," Su said.

I turned. "A wolf? Haven't you had enough of wolves lately?"

"I want to be a wolf," she said.

"Su—"

"That's doable," Winter said, suddenly entering the room. "Nothing wrong with it."

"I didn't say there was anything wrong with it," I said. But it *did* hit me wrong, what with how Su had acted when real wolves stalked our yard. "I'll go get the box." I stepped forward and nearly ran right into Ethan. He stepped quickly aside and I blundered past, but not before my nose caught the full scent of him. I hurried to the top of the stairs and ducked into the doorway of my and Su's room. I took several deep breaths: Ethan smelled in such a way that made me long to bury my face in the nape of his neck—it was a warm smell, oddly familiar, slightly musky and slightly wild like a warm, clean animal. I'd asked Emma, in school the previous day, if she ever noticed the way guys smell. "Like when they come off the basketball court?" she'd said.

"No—I mean when they smell good."

"You mean like Jack's great Axe experiment?"

"No—not that, either. Like when just the way they smell—*them*, not cologne or anything—when there's just something about the way they smell that draws you to them."

"Oh," Emma'd said. "You mean like pheromones and things like that?"

"Pheromones?"

"Body chemistry."

"I guess I mean something like that," I'd said.

"Some people are just attracted to the way other people smell."

"Oh."

We had stopped at my locker. Emma looked around as I did the combination, then she leaned closer to me. "Does Ethan smell good?" she'd asked.

"Ethan? How would I know?" I'd felt color rushing to my cheeks, and I'd hoped she wouldn't notice.

"Well, you sort of live with him—I thought maybe you'd notice."

"I try not to," I'd said. That was true enough.

She leaned back against the locker next to mine and looked off at nothing. "He looks like he'd smell good," she'd said. "You should talk him into coming out with us on Halloween."

She'd smiled as she said that, but something was off, something I couldn't quite put my finger on. It was more a feeling than a thought:

what? "I'll try," I'd said.

Now, in my room, I caught my breath and pulled out the dusty box of material from under Su's bed, taking it downstairs to the living room.

We spent the rest of that afternoon and the whole of that evening working on costumes—or a costume, I should say; Winter and I both worked on Su's costume as I resigned myself to the thought of digging out my witch costume from two Halloweens ago. It was your plain classic black witch costume: a big black hat and a black wool cape which I'd made out of an old wool blanket that I'd cut and dyed. It was a warm costume. That was my consolation. That and the fact that I do look good in black.

Su's costume ended up consisting of a big gray fuzzy wool sweater and mittens, some black fleece pants, a tail from a piece of faux fur trim and a gray knit hat with black felt ears. It wasn't genius but it would do. Su seemed pleased enough. "Where's Ethan?" she asked as she stood in front of us. "I want him to see this!"

"Right here." And Ethan was there, suddenly, leaning in the doorway of the living room.

Su faltered. She hadn't wanted him to hear. I watched helplessly as her cheeks flushed and she tried to find the right words.

"Great! You're here," I said quickly. "We've been wanting you to see this—what do you think?"

He looked at me. I smiled at him but did not meet his eyes. I then looked toward Su, still in the middle of the living room.

Ethan said, about the costume: "It's good."

"Yeah?" Su's face lit up. "What are you going to be?"

"Me? I wasn't planning on being anything," he said.

I could see Su's face fall—we all, I think, saw Su's face fall. "Maybe it is kind of silly," she said. "Halloween."

"Not so silly, Su," Ethan said quickly. "The blurring of boundaries between worlds."

Su's face eased. "So will you come with us?"

He looked at Winter and something passed between them.

"Okay," he said. "But no costume." He scratched at the side of his nose in a nervous, twitchy sort of way. Then he left the room

☽

Halloween—which was also Keats' birthday—dawned gray and

cold. It was a day that promised neither snow nor sun, just gray, winter-cold gray. But the temperature stayed low and by the time we got home from school the day felt heavy and bleak. I went up to my room and looked out my window. Then I saw the tracks in the snow.

Even from my window I could see they didn't belong to Keats. It hadn't been that long since the wolves were here, but I had nearly forgotten them, my mind on other things. I quietly glided down the stairs and slipped on my boots and coat. Keats stood at the ready, waiting to go outside with me, but I disappointed him. "I'll be back in a minute," I told him. "You hang tight and then I'll take you out." I remembered it was his birthday and I gave him a kiss before I pulled the wooden latch on the door and stepped outside into the cold.

The tracks were a single set and circled—though from a slight distance—Ethan's cabin, and I determined they were made either last night or early this morning. There was one spot where they seemed to lean in toward Ethan's doorway, but there was a space of at least three feet of unmarked snow. I pictured the wolf in my mind: large and silent, graceful and knowing. Knowing that we were asleep in our houses. Knowing that he or she could slip like a ghost into our territory and not waken us, could be here with us unknowing. I walked past Ethan's cabin and paused, wondering if I should knock and let him know I was out here. I opted not to disturb him and refocused on the tracks, trying to find where the wolf had originally come out of the woods. My head was bent and my eyes were concentrated on the ground when I heard a voice say: "He came from this way. Over here."

I looked up and saw Dangerous Dan, an oversized rifle slung over his shoulder, standing at the edge of the woods. I straightened and wondered what to say. I knew what I *wanted* to say—I wanted him off our land—but I also didn't want to be overly rude. I didn't want there to be "something" between us.

"My dogs are going crazy," Dan said. "I've got to catch this son-of-a-bitch." His jaw flexed as he spoke.

"Has it been around your house?"

"Some."

"Just one?"

"Just one this week. Last week there was a whole pack. But they just passed through."

"Well," I said, "this one's probably just passing through, too."

"Seems to be hanging around to me."

I didn't respond.

"I've seen the tracks—every morning now for a week."

"I haven't," I said.

"Well, I have. Ever since the last snow. He's hanging around, so he must be looking for food or something. My dogs are going crazy at night, and I'm just waiting. I've got some traps out, and I'll get 'em."

"Traps!" I said. "Where?"

"Round my place. In the woods, too, between here and there."

I felt the color rise in my cheeks. "This is a neighborhood," I said. "People have dogs."

"Well, they'd better keep their dogs home safe or on a line or something. They don't need to be running around, either."

With that he pulled on his gun strap so that his rifle—which had been gradually tipping backwards—straightened on his shoulder, and he turned around in those big green boots of his and walked away. When I turned, I saw Ethan looking out the front window of the guest cabin. But only for a second. I kept my eyes from looking that way as I passed by again. Then I hurried back into the house, a chill from the freezing air following me inside.

Winter was in the kitchen now, working on a sketch, and she looked up when she heard me open the door.

"Tri!" she said. "Where were you?"

"There are more wolf tracks," I said.

Something crossed over her face. I wasn't sure what. "Oh," she said. "You sure?"

"Yes."

"One set?"

"Yes."

"Oh—well, that's all right then."

"One wolf is still one wolf," I said. "We usually don't have wolves like this." But as I said that I remembered something. I remembered sitting up in my bed at night, cold and crying and hearing howling outside. I remember my father coming into the room and holding me.

Why are there wolves, Daddy?

Why is there anything, Tri?

But why are they here?

Because they like us, Tri. That's all. They like us and they want to visit us.

But why do they like us?

Because. . .because. . .

Had he ever answered that question? "They're not here because they like us," I said out loud.

"What?" Winter asked.

"I said they're not here because they like us. My dad used to say that, when we were little, that the wolves were here because they liked us. So we did have wolves—sometimes. But they haven't been around like this for a long time. And now Dan's out setting traps!"

Winter had started making coffee and now she just stood, looking at me. "What did you say?"

"I said now Dan's out setting traps. Between here and his place."

"How do you know that?"

"He just told me." I let her wait a minute. "He was here, out by the guest cabin. I went to look at the tracks and there he was, lurking in the woods."

"Oh," she said, the word sounding like a heavy weight. "Great. Well, we're just going to have to find them and spring them."

"He'll get mad if we do that." Winter knew as well as I did that he would be able to tell who did it, that he would track us back to our house.

Winter chewed on her bottom lip and didn't say anything else. Keats was whining at the door, and I opened it to let him out.

"Don't do that!" Winter said. "I mean go with him. Keep him in the yard and bring him right back."

"Okay," I said, though not without resentment. I did promise Keats I'd take him out, but someone else could do it once in a while. I opened the door and he rushed into the cold air. He peed on a variety of things (the right front tire of the Subaru, a poor small helpless baby spruce tree, Su's bicycle, which she hadn't put away yet for the winter) before finding the wolf tracks. I expected him to growl or shake or something—but he just sniffed and followed, circling the guest cabin, as if he knew for sure the wolf was long gone. I didn't know for sure, and I kept a cautious watch.

Then Ethan emerged. He saw me right away, and his eyes met mine for an instant then he watched as Keats stopped, then carefully approached him. Ethan put out a gentle hand and stroked the top of Keats' head. But Keats backed away from him at that, turning and coming back to me. "There are more wolf tracks," I said.

Ethan's eyes darted in the direction of the tracks as if he already knew they were there. He was wearing a wool sweater and a pair of mittens. "I was going to split some wood," he said, still looking at the tracks.

"You don't have to do that." I wondered what would happen this time if a wolf showed up by the woodshed.

"I know that," he said, "but I want to." Then he added, "I know what it's like to have a lot of chores." I looked at him, and our eyes met as he stood there in the gray light, his hair moving in the cold quiet breeze. For the first time in my life, I had the feeling that someone *saw* me—not as grumpy Tri or serious Tri but Tri who just ended up taking care of things: me. Me. "Thanks," I said. He smiled quietly and looked up at the sky. I waited a moment, watching his face, then asked, "What are you looking at?"

"Nothing," he said. "And everything. Listen."

I looked upwards and listened. I heard birds—chickadees—somewhere in the trees. A happy sound. There was a slight breeze and the soft whisper of it moving through the trees. When I looked back at Ethan, he was looking at me. Suddenly the day, this ordinary gray day, seemed beautiful. Was it because Ethan was there, with his glossy curls and his slender shoulders, or was it because I had simply stopped long enough to see it right? I managed a weak smile then said, "C'mon Keats," and reluctantly headed toward the door. A second later I looked quickly back over my shoulder. Ethan was crouched now close to the thin layer of snow, studying the ribbon of tracks.

Later, as the last of the light slipped from the sky, we were all four of us in the kitchen, drinking coffee and tea while Winter cooked caribou steaks for Ethan and Su and I heated a small pot of vegetable soup for myself. I was somehow reminded about the way my dad would sometimes eat a caribou steak or a moose steak for breakfast; I do remember that. I wondered if that was something I would soon be re-experiencing: the smell of meat in the morning, not something I enjoyed. I leaned against the wall and looked out the window as I waited for my soup. I could sense Ethan's dark eyes glancing at me. I was feeling worried, and I was feeling tired of feeling worried. Even the nearness of Ethan couldn't distract me out of it this dark early evening—Halloween evening. The worst thing was I didn't know what I was worried about, specifically—the wolves, the traps, Ethan and Su. It was more like this strange feeling that we were vulnerable, somehow, our odd little family, like a small boat on the ocean: if the wind didn't blow too hard, if the water didn't rise too much, if the boat held tight.

A lot of ifs.

When my soup was ready, I poured it into a bowl and grabbed a spoon. Then I quietly left the room with it, three sets of dark eyes watching me go.

Seven

It was dark, cold, and we were on an unlit street. Su, Ethan, and Jack were ahead of me; Emma had been with them, too, but noticed how I hung back and slowed to join me.

"You okay?" she asked.

"Yes—I'm fine." I kept looking at the shadowy trees that lurked in the borders of the near-houseless street, sweeping the blackness with my flashlight. "I'm just cold." I had forgotten to put a headband on under my witch hat and my ears were freezing, so that was partly true. But I was noticing how Ethan and Su walked closely together.

Emma's green alien antennae bobbed as she walked, and even in the darkness I thought I could see the sting of the cold on her small nose. "It is cold," she said. "It must be nice down in the states—Halloween, you know."

"You'd know better than me," I said.

"It was definitely warmer," she said. I could tell she had noticed the edge in my voice. She added, "I didn't mean to make it sound like I'd always been here or anything."

"I know," I said. I smiled. Then I noticed again how close Ethan was walking with Su. I didn't look away fast enough, and Emma noticed me noticing.

"What is that?" she asked quietly.

I hesitated, then said, "I don't know."

"Her costume came out good."

"Thanks."

As if he heard our near-whispers, Ethan turned and looked back at us, but only for a fraction of a second. His pale face glowed in the dark. Then he seemed to pick up his pace, and Su's legs worked to keep up.

It was Jack who waited and joined me and Emma at our slower pace. I realized the cemetery was nearby. Up ahead, Ethan and Su rounded a bend as the street curved around it. My eyes strained in the

53

darkness. I felt suddenly anxious and picked up the pace. As we came around the bend Su was standing so still in our path that we almost ran into her.

"Su!" I said. She was staring off toward the cemetery. I followed her gaze but couldn't see anything except layers of darkness. "Where's Ethan?"

Su looked at me for a moment, her face open and confused. "He just started running."

"Running? Where?"

She nodded toward the gated cemetery, with its shadowy hodgepodge of crosses and tombstones. "Something was in there."

I felt Emma and Jack close. "What do you mean, Su?" I asked quietly, my voice barely above a whisper.

"Something was in there. I could feel it. And Ethan could, too. I could hear it breathing!"

"Su—"

"And then he ran in there. Tri, you've never seen anyone run so fast!"

We stood frozen on the silent street, staring at the cemetery. Emma and I looked at each other. Jack peered hard through the darkness. "Let me see the flashlight," he said. "I'll go take a look."

"No, Jack, I'll go," I said.

"Maybe we should just stick together," Emma suggested, and as a group we moved slowly forward across the street to the cemetery gates. I shined the flashlight across the quiet grounds, lightly coated with the frozen remains of the first snows. Nothing. There was nothing. We yelled and waited, then yelled again. Nothing.

"We should just go to the Altitude," Emma said. "Ethan knew we were going to go there."

I nodded, and we backed away, making a silent and methodical retreat back the way we came.

At the Altitude I called Winter from the payphone by the restrooms. "Ethan's gone," I said.

"What happened?" Winter sounded calm.

"I don't know. He and Su were up ahead and when we caught up, he was gone. Su said they heard something in the cemetery, and he ran off."

There was a slight pause. "Okay," she said. "Well, don't worry about it, Tri. I'll take a look around before I come pick you up."

"Okay," I said.

"All right then," Winter said. "I'll see you soon!"

"Okay." I hung up the phone.

"What did she say?" Emma hovered nearby.

"Not much," I said. "She didn't seem too worried."

We exchanged a look, then rejoined Jack and Su at a table.

"We ordered cocoa and fries," Su said quietly. I could see the anxiousness on her face.

"What did your stepmom say?" Jack asked.

"She said don't worry," I said and sat down. We didn't say much. Our fries came, and our cocoa came, and Jack's parents came and he left, then Emma's dad came and she left, too, and when Winter finally came for us there was still no sign of Ethan.

☽

Later, at home, I took Keats out for a short walk in honor of his birthday, keeping him on a leash for fear of Dan's traps. Winter kept acting like everything was okay, but I think she was just waiting for me and Su to go to bed. Maybe Ethan was simply weird, I thought, or maybe he *was* into drugs. Our village was not without drugs and druggies. Maybe he'd made some new friends that we didn't know about.

Keats was sniffing the ground, and he pulled me toward the woods. I looked over my shoulder at the lighted house, glowing warm and familiar in the dark as I let Keats drag me along on whatever quest he was on.

He kept going, and he started going faster. He's a big dog, and he wasn't listening to me when I tried to make him turn back toward the house. Before I knew it, I was sprinting behind him, the trees growing thicker and everything growing darker.

Then suddenly Keats stopped. And I heard growling. It took me a moment to realize it was Keats.

I pulled on the leash. "C'mon, Keats, time to go home," I whispered, my eyes searching in the direction he was staring. "C'mon." But he wouldn't budge.

Then I saw what he saw and my blood stilled. There was the head of a wolf, low to the ground near the base of a spruce, eyes reflective even in the black dark. And as this presence registered in my brain I realized there were two layers of sound in the growling I heard: growls from Keats' throat, and from that of the wolf's. The wolf was looking at me and for a moment its growling stopped. But then it looked again at Keats and its lips curled back in a snarl and in an instant Keats lunged forward, snapping me off my feet as the leash whipped tight. "Keats! No!" I screamed as I fell and hit the hard earth, my hand still gripping tightly on his leash. Keats yelped. I didn't realize he had stopped his attack—and there was no attack from the wolf—until I pulled myself up from the ground and flung my arms around his big neck and chest in an effort to save him from what I thought would be certain doom. But he was still, and when I looked up there was no wolf but a naked Ethan sprawled on the frozen ground. I couldn't comprehend what I was seeing. Where did he come from? Where were his clothes? Where was the wolf? And as these thoughts whirled across my mind my eyes shifted through the darkness and followed the length of Ethan's outstretched form to where his foot lay twisted and bloody in the steel jaws of a trap.

"Oh my God," I said. "Oh, God." I felt as if I was losing my mind.

But Ethan looked at me and I saw how he shook. It was well below freezing, he had no clothes on, and he was hurt. I dropped Keats' leash and tore off my wool witch's cape, draping it over Ethan. I grabbed the trap and his face twisted with pain. The trap had steel teeth which had sunk deeply into his flesh and bone. I didn't have any light. Then I noticed Keats turn his head slightly and I saw at once what he saw: a bright beam moving through the woods. A flashlight. Dan, out checking the area, possibly out checking his traps. His dogs were barking—frantic sounding, like they were either excited or afraid or both. Quickly I felt down the chain of the trap and found where it was nailed to the tree. I pulled. I pulled some more, working the ring at the end of the chain. I could feel the nail, which was looped over the ring, loosen and I was able to turn it and I found a little dip in the wood. I popped the ring free.

"We have to get out of here, Ethan," I said. I simultaneously helped him move and broke a branch off the tree which I used to try to sweep away our tracks. I prayed for snow. I prayed for Dan to turn back toward his house. The light still bobbed in the trees, but it remained a ways off. Maybe he wasn't going to come this far, this close to our house, tonight. With the witch's cape draped over him and the trap dangling painfully from the end of his foot, Ethan leaned on me and I rushed him as best as I could through the dark forest, Keats my only light.

Eight

A while later I sat in the dark of my room by my window, looking out at the night, waiting for morning to come, waiting for the light to weave its way into the blackness and bring familiarity back to the shadows and unknown shapes that had crept and crawled into my world, crowding it with uncertainty and mystery. Something was wrong. That was the only thing I knew for certain; everything else was filmy and shrouded—unknown.

Su slept quietly in her bed—had slept quietly through it all. Su was the first thing Winter had thought of, when Ethan and I came crashing through the door, blood trickling steadily from his wounded foot. At once her finger went to her mouth, making clear the need to be quiet. Together we took Ethan into the living room and sat him down by the fire. Winter began briskly rubbing his cold skin. "Tri," she whispered, "bring a bowl of hot water, clean towels, and washcloths. The first aid kit. Put the kettle on."

I did what she said. When I returned, a puddle of blood had grown on the floor. Winter took a towel and placed it beneath Ethan's wounded foot. "Keep him still," she told me. I looked at Ethan, who shook in the chair. His eyes found mine and all his pain, his fear, and his aloneness shuddered through my soul. In that instant I knew something: I *knew* him somehow—I knew him. Or that's what it felt like.

Then Winter pried open the jaws of the trap and Ethan's eyes tore away as his mouth opened to cry out. But I slammed my forearm between his teeth and for that moment we were united in pain as his teeth sank into my flesh.

"Tri—I need you. Now." Winter's voice was firm and flat and calm. Ethan loosened his grip on my arm and looked at me in horror as blood oozed from the bite marks in my skin. I shook my head, wanting to say, *Don't worry,* but out of the corner of my eye I could see the blood pouring now from his foot and Winter's hands rushing to stop it.

"Should we call an ambulance?" I asked, my voice shaking with fear.

"No—peroxide," she said. I grabbed the bottle and screwed off the lid. She poured it onto Ethan's wounded foot and it bubbled and fizzed as it mixed with the blood. "There's a needle and some floss. Thread the needle, Tri, hurry." My hands shook as I fumbled through the first aid kit. Somehow, I found the needle and threaded it; somehow, I did it. "Hold the towel here," Winter instructed. "Try to keep pressure on." I did as she said and tried not to look as she began stitching a wound on the top of his foot. I felt his eyes on me. Cautiously I met his stare. He still shook and he winced as Winter's needle slipped in and out of his skin, but his mouth stayed closed, and his eyes stayed on me. Then it was done, and Winter closed the other wounds with butterfly bandages before wrapping his foot in clean white gauze. Ethan's breathing slowly steadied and I watched him fight to keep his eyes open before he succumbed to sleep.

"Will he be all right?" I whispered.

Winter nodded. She looked at the bloody floor and shook her head, seeming lost for a few moments in a world of her own. But when her eyes lifted they registered on my bitten arm, and a look I will never forget swept across her face. "He bit you!" she whispered fiercely.

"He didn't mean—"

"No!"

"It's okay—"

"No! No!" And to my horror she pulled her pocketknife from out of the pocket of her jeans, grabbed me firmly by the arm and swiftly cut through the teeth marks with the sharp little blade.

"Winter! What are you doing?"

"We have to. . .we have to. . .get the germs out, Tri—I'm so sorry!"

The pain shot through me and blood was spilling from my arm, falling onto the floor where it mixed with Ethan's. I looked at Winter in disbelief.

She looked me firmly in the eyes. "Listen, Tri, listen to me. Everything is all right. Everything will be all right. Ethan—"

"There's something wrong with him, isn't there?"

"He has—he has an affliction, Tri. A—malady." Her voice was shaky and urgent.

"He's sick?"

"Yes—yes, he's sick. It's something that runs in my family. I have it, too, and see? I'm all right. But Ethan needs help right now. He needs our help, Tri."

"Why did you cut me?"

"Oh, sweetheart, it was just to make sure the germs didn't get into you."

"So he's contiguous?"

She didn't answer.

"Does he have AIDS?"

"No, no, honey, nothing like that."

"Then what?"

"Just an. . .affliction."

"In the woods—I saw something." I was trying to sort it out. What did I see? There was a wolf, then there was Ethan. Ethan with no clothes. "I saw a wolf," I said. "Then Ethan was there."

"Well, you saved him then."

"From what?"

"The wolf."

"Wolves don't—they don't typically attack people, Winter. You know that."

"There are always exceptions to everything, Tri." She had poured peroxide over my wound and was bandaging it tightly. She was lying to me. I felt that as sure as I felt the cuts on my arm.

"Is he dangerous?"

"Ethan? No—no, he's not dangerous."

"Su was outside with him, a couple of nights ago. She acts like she doesn't remember it, but I saw her."

"He won't hurt her, Tri."

"What if he—they—"

"He won't do anything to Su, Tri."

"But he's always watching her."

"It's not like that, Tri. It's not. Can't you tell?"

"Tell what?"

She looked me full in the face. "It's you, Tri."

"It's me what?"

"It's you that haunts his heart."

Our conversation had ended there. I went upstairs, leaving Winter in the living room watching over Ethan, but I could not sleep. A short time later I saw Winter slip out the back door, and in the light from the window I could see the sinister trap dangling from her hand. She was going to return it, I knew: somehow, she would find the right tree in that dark army of trees. A seemingly short time later she returned, and it looked like she was carrying something, maybe Ethan's clothes.

I knew she was lying to me and I didn't know why. And the scene in the woods kept playing over and over in my mind: Keats, the wolf, Keats, then Ethan. Where had he gone when he ran through the cemetery? How did he end up without any clothes? Why did Winter cut my arm?

It's you that haunts his heart. Winter's words rose up through the chaos in my mind and echoed through me. Did I? Could I believe that— could I believe anything? Eventually I crawled into my bed, and sometime during that long night I fell asleep.

I dreamed of wolves. And of Ethan. That we were walking together through an open, grassy area and it was summer. His dark eyes looked sideways at me, and on his lips was something like a smile. Then I saw, low in the grass, pairs of eyes, eyes all around us, watching. Wolves. I wanted to tell him but I couldn't; my voice wouldn't work. Then suddenly it was winter, frosty and snowy, all blue and white and gray and Ethan stood in front of me. He bent his head and pressed it against the top of my shoulder, then I woke up to the sound of a knocking on the door.

I crept down the stairs. Winter crouched silently in the threshold to the living room, and she motioned for me to be quiet. Her hand was firmly around Keats' muzzle, but I could see she wouldn't be able to hold him long. The knocking kept coming. Then Keats broke free and pushed himself against the door to the entryway, barking as if every monster that ever existed waited outside.

That might have seemed a bit easier than dealing with Dan. Winter nodded for me to answer the door, and she slipped back into the living room, shrouded in the soft light of the morning.

"Good morning, Trileka," Dan said when I opened the door.

"Hello."

"Bet you're wondering why I'm here so early on a Saturday."

I shrugged. But I noticed that his lips were trembling and his nostrils were quivering.

"One of my dogs was *murdered* last night! Torn to bits while trapped on his chain." I could see how he struggled to keep himself under control.

"That's terrible, Dan."

"It was wolves!"

"Really?"

"Two of them!"

"Two?"

"Well, there are two different sets of tracks. And those tracks lead here! Well, one set does."

"Here?"

"All the wolf tracks lead back to here, Trileka, and I can't for the life of me figure out why! You got some wolf radar thing going on or something?"

"Some what?" I could just play dumb, which would probably fit with what I imagined Dan's perception of women was.

"It doesn't make any sense. And they're different tracks, too—where are all these wolves coming from?"

"I don't know."

"Why now?"

"I don't know."

"And why would they kill my dog? A dog on a chain is helpless, you know. All I heard was one yelp. One yelp. Then silence. They—it, whatever—tore out his throat. Just tore it out. And then left. Left for here."

"Keats didn't notice anything."

"Do you want to see the tracks? There's blood, too, here and there on the snow. Where is Winter? Is she not up yet?"

"I'm here, Dan." Winter's voice emerged from behind me. "Tri, you can go on back upstairs."

"All right," I said, but I lingered halfway up.

"Dan, I'm really sorry about your dog," Winter said. "But it's kind of upsetting to me that you would come lay all that on Tri—and she hasn't even had a chance to wake up yet. She doesn't need to hear the gory details of your dog's death."

There was a pause. Then Dan said, "You're right, Winter, I apologize."

"And you keep coming around here acting like we've got something to do with this sudden wolf problem!"

"You're right. It's just that—"

"Wolves are wild creatures, Dan. We don't have any wolves for pets. You know our pet. His name is Keats."

"Yes, you're right—I didn't mean—"

"Have you been reading some mysteries-of-the-north type books? Maybe some supernatural thrillers?"

"No, I—"

"Well, quit acting like we're a bunch of werewolves or something. We're just as freaked out about theses wolves as you are, and except for my nephew Ethan it's just me and these girls here."

"I'm sorry, Winter, I didn't mean—it's just, well, I guess I'm a little freaked out myself now. . .and. . ."

"It's all right, Dan."

I left at that and continued up the stairs. Su was coverless, curled in a ball on her bed.

I gave her a nudge. "Weren't you going to Samantha's today?" I asked. Then her head snapped up, teeth barred, and I jumped away.

She laughed. I put my hand over my heart. "What is wrong with you?" I asked.

"Tri! Lighten up! I'm just playing with you!" Somehow her voice seemed lower. She rolled out of bed and gave a long stretch. "It's funny how time flies when you're sleeping!" Then she slunk past me and pulled open the curtains. A low, growly sound came from her throat. I looked past her shoulder and saw Dan walking away, sad and dejected, his big gun slopping on his shoulder. When he was a safe distance Su pulled open the window and began sniffing the air.

"Good morning!"

I turned and Winter was in the doorway. "Su, go downstairs and make some coffee, would you?" she said.

"Ohhhh," Su moaned, and pulled herself away from the window. "Why is that always my job?"

"Come on now," Winter said. "You know Tri usually does it."

"Ohhh," Su moaned again. Winter caught her in the doorway and handed her a flannel robe. Her nightgown, worn and old, seemed especially thin this morning.

"What's wrong with her?" I whispered as soon as Su was gone. Winter put her finger to her lips.

"There's nothing wrong with me, Tri!" Su's voice rang up from the bottom of the stairs and I couldn't figure out how she'd heard me. Again Winter put her finger to her lips. When we heard Su banging around in the kitchen, Winter came close and said, "There's nothing wrong." Again I could tell she was lying. Her eyes kept darting to Su's messed up bed. "How did you sleep last night?" she asked.

"Not very good."

"And how's the arm?" She seemed to be studying my face.

"It's okay. What do you think happened to Dan's dog?"

"I don't know."

"Maybe the wolves?"

"Maybe."

Then we heard something like a cry coming from the living room, and Winter and I hurried down the stairs.

"He's hurt!" Su said as we rushed into the room where we found her on the floor at Ethan's feet. "He's hurt!"

"We know that, Su!" I said. "We know that already!"

"But no one told me!"

"You were sleeping!"

"You didn't want me to know!"

"Why wouldn't I want to you know?" I said, but then I remembered that we did, indeed, keep it from her on purpose.

"You know why, Tri." Again her voice sounded deeper. I felt the hair stand up on my forearms. Then I noticed that all their eyes—Winter's, Su's, and Ethan's—were on me. I felt a strange chill run through me. I backed out of the room.

$$\mathcal{D}$$

The day was long and slow. I spent much of it alone in the kitchen, painfully aware that Su was in the living room, curled close to Ethan on the couch. Once when I went up to my room I startled Winter, who was changing the sheets on Su's bed.

I gave her a quizzical look. That wasn't normal behavior.

"I'll do yours tomorrow," she said quickly.

"That's okay," I said. "Mine don't need it."

Winter smiled, finished the bed, and left the room. I looked at Su's covers, lifted assorted corners and wondered what it was, what it was that made Winter change the sheets. But there was nothing—at least nothing that was still there.

I slept little. I tried not to sleep at all.

Sunday morning I crept slowly down the stairs. On my way to the kitchen I froze, the hair on the back of my neck tingling. I looked down the hallway and there was Ethan, leaning against the back door. He didn't look well and seemed to be breathing strangely.

"Ethan," I said, rushing over. "Are you okay?" He was sweaty and pale. I touched his forehead and when I did a jolt of something ran through me and I felt my knees tremble from it.

He grabbed my arm. "I bit you," he said.

"It's okay. It's not bad."

"No," he said. "It's *not* okay, Tri—I *bit* you." His voice was whispery and ragged. He was shaking his head, and his dark eyes looked watery as if with tears.

"It's okay. Really."

"No—you don't understand." He grabbed the doorknob with a sweaty hand. "I have to leave."

"You're sick," I said. "You should lie down. . ."

He seemed dizzy and I grabbed him. Then his arms wrapped tight around me, and he pressed his forehead against my shoulder. "Tri. . ." he said, "Tri."

"Ethan," I whispered. I closed my eyes. My hands found his hair. Suddenly Ethan—the feel of him, the smell of him—was all that there was. For a brief moment I didn't care about anything else. For a brief moment. Then from somewhere behind me I heard Su yelling for Winter, her voice angry-sounding, and then Winter was there, gently prying Ethan away from me, taking him back to the living room. I pressed my back against the wall and let myself slide down to the floor. I closed my eyes and touched the side of my face where his skin had touched mine. I felt dizzy with—something. Then I felt a strange tingling, like someone was watching me. I opened my eyes and there was Su, staring at me fiercely, looking almost as if she hated me. Then she ran off, and I pulled myself upright, feeling as if I was tumbling down a hill with nothing to grab onto.

Again the day passed painfully slowly. I tunneled into myself, refusing to think. Ethan returned to the guest cabin. Su began acting normally again; it was as if I had imagined everything. But I hadn't. If nothing else there was the bite on my arm and the wounds in Ethan's foot.

That night I couldn't help myself and slept. When Monday morning came I felt almost normal, though still exhausted despite the sleep, and I didn't even care that both Ethan and Su weren't feeling up for school. I was. I was up for school. I wanted a normal day.

But shortly after I got on the bus, *they* got on. Two boys—new boys, strangers. Wade and Jake James. Brothers. Strangers. And as they emerged from the frosty semi-light and climbed through the doorway Mr. Palmer opened up for them, they looked right at me as if they knew me, and they sat down in the seat behind me and I felt the skin on the back of my neck begin to tingle.

Nine

"Can you believe this? Three new boys in one month! It's like a whole new lease on school life! How could we get so lucky?" Emma's voice hissed in a loud whisper. She claimed to be very happy, but I wondered if she really was. It wasn't like her to get giddy over boys. A few minutes previously Chris Evans had walked by our table and said hi to us. Emma had shot him a glance and didn't respond, turning the talk quickly to the boys I had seen emerge from the morning. "And they seem to notice us, too, Tri."

We were at lunch in the student center. Wade and Jake James were three tables away, sitting side by side and facing our direction. The rest of their table was empty. I noticed that nobody was attempting to befriend the new duo. It was as if an energy field of some sort surrounded them, keeping others at bay.

There *was* something strange about them that I couldn't put my finger on. But it was the same sort of strangeness that seemed to surround Ethan—a whisper of something, something you couldn't put into words.

I still hadn't told Emma what had happened Halloween night and I didn't know if I should. I still didn't know what *had* happened.

"Which one do you think is cuter, Tri?"

"I don't know," I said, trying to be disinterested but not so much as to arouse Emma's suspicion. I wanted everything new and strange to just go away. But that would mean Ethan, I realized, and the memory of him touching me in the hall sent firecrackers off in my stomach. How could I want him to go away?

"I think Jake must be the older one," Emma said. As she spoke, I swore I could see a flicker shoot across Jake's face as I tried not to look at him.

"Shh," I said.

"They can't hear us." Emma dropped her voice to a whisper.

"You never know."

"Tri, they can't possibly hear us."

But I sensed that they could. I felt Jake's eerie white-blue eyes dart in my direction. I opened my notebook to a blank page, scribbled a sentence and slid it over to Emma: *Let's write instead. It'll be like old times—remember ninth grade?*

Emma smiled and picked up her pencil. *Who wants to remember that?*

Only in retrospect, I thought.

So—which one—Jake or Wade? Emma wrote.

Who do you think is cute? I wondered what she would really say, if she felt she could. Would she say, *Chris Evans—remember him?*

Wade.

Why?

He's not all wolf-like. Jake looks like a wolf. He's creepy. Well, maybe. But really, I guess he's kind of cute, too. In a wolf kind of way.

My stomach twisted as I read her words. Jake did have a lean and hungry look, his ball-cap pulled down low across his forehead, emphasizing the sharp angles of his pointy face. Wade's face was rounder, but in my mind he, too, had a wolf-like look; he was fairer and broader-shouldered than Jake, but had the same strange eyes. Was I simply going crazy from the stress of all the recent wolf activity? Or better yet—was this whole last stretch of my life just a dream, and would I wake up tomorrow to find everything as it always had been?

But if this was a dream, for now I was still in it. And the way out had not yet revealed itself to me.

"What happened to your arm?" Emma asked.

My sleeve had ridden up my forearm, exposing the bandages. "Nothing," I said.

"Tri—"

"Keats accidentally nipped me." I hated lying. Again I sensed that the brothers were listening.

"Keats? Really? That's hard to believe!"

"He's upset these days."

"About what?" The tone of her voice now echoed the scowl that had crossed her face.

"Wolves," I said.

And I could hear them, those brothers, across the small span of space that separated us; I could hear them laughing. I slowly moved my eyes. They were looking right at me, and for an instant I returned

Jake James' icy stare. Then he and his brother rose and left the lunchroom. My skin was tingling and I felt alert and alive.

"What's wrong, Tri?" Emma asked.

"Nothing," I said. I watched the brothers disappear down the hall.

Sometime later the bell finally rang and the school day was over. I had fallen asleep in my last class of the afternoon, but no one seemed to notice. I felt heavy and almost drugged as I tried to pull myself awake. In the hall I struggled with my locker combo, and after I got it, the door was stuck again. I pulled weakly on the handle. Then a strong looking arm in a gray sweatshirt crossed my line of vision and a manly, nicely shaped hand effortlessly opened it. I looked up into the face of Wade James, who smiled down at me. I felt a tingling on the back of my neck. Without a word, and as silently as he had appeared, he walked away.

I could smell him. It was a familiar smell: a smell like a fast-running winter stream or a crisp field of tall wild ferns. Or like clean fur.

"Aren't you the one." Emma appeared at my side, her eyes following Wade James down the hall. "Are all the new guys going to go after you? You have some new perfume or something?"

I could not answer. I walked numbly out of the school and turned toward my bus. Then I *felt* them coming up behind me; I felt them. I instantly remembered Su saying how she could *feel* the wolves. What was happening to us?

As they passed me, they came closer to me than they needed to, so close that Wade's arm brushed my shoulder.

He turned. "Sorry," he said.

I looked at him and my eyes met his. Something crossed his face; it was almost like he wanted to say something. Then his eyes slid down to the bandage on my arm right before his brother grabbed him by the shirtsleeve and jerked him away.

When I got home, Aunt Tabby was in the living room with Winter and Su. Keats was happily lying by the fire. I didn't see Ethan.

Sydney had met me at the bus stop; instantly I had thought something was wrong, but he assured me all was well. "Something eating you, Muzzy?" he'd asked, using the slang for mosquito from his native Australia. I shook my head and swallowed down everything that threatened to spill from my mouth. I didn't want Sydney to know the thoughts I was thinking.

"Hi," I said now, entering the house and pretending to feel normal. Everyone was smiling, then suddenly Tabby and Winter weren't. They looked at me then looked at each other. Su seemed oblivious.

"Anything happen?" Su asked, meaning at school.

"There were some new boys," I said.

"Really? Who? Are they cute?"

As I started to tell her what little I knew I felt something—someone—behind me. I thought at first it was Sydney but then I smelled him. I looked over my shoulder. Ethan was looking at the sleeve of my fleece jacket, then he looked at Winter. I realized he'd been staring at the area where Wade James had brushed up against me. Winter rose and came over to me, smiling a smile that didn't look like a real smile to me.

"Here, Tri," she said. "Let me take your things so you can go talk to Su." She gently grabbed my backpack and pulled my jacket down off my shoulders. Tabby rose and crossed the room and stood beside Winter. "There," Winter said. "Go on in and sit down. We'll go make everyone some cocoa."

Before I could respond Sydney came in through the entryway, juggling some grocery bags. "You're off dinner duty tonight, Tri," he said. Mondays were among my nights to cook. "I've got it all taken care of."

"So you have," said Tabby, who then took the bags from him. "But Winter and I are going into the kitchen now, to make cocoa and get things a little organized for you, so go on in, love, and have a seat with Tri and Su for a few minutes."

"Oh—all right," Sydney said. Obediently we walked into the living room. I noticed they took my jacket into the kitchen. I noticed Ethan followed them.

I stayed by the doorway and soon felt eyes on me and there was Ethan, in that small space between the living room and the kitchen, standing awkwardly with his bandaged foot and a home-made crutch I recognized as one Winter had made when once she'd sprained her ankle. I felt pulled toward him, and before I knew it, I was standing close to him and our eyes were locked. I reached over and opened the door to the entryway, and we slid into its cool darkness.

He dropped the crutch and fell against me, again pressing his forehead onto my shoulder. My heart thundered in my chest. I tried to remember to breathe.

"Don't go to him," he whispered, his breath against my neck.

"Who?" I flashed on Wade James, brushing up against me. My brain spun. How could Ethan know?

Then he touched the side of his face against mine, and without another word he let go of me and slipped back inside. Alone in the dank coolness of the entryway I tried to steady my breathing. I sniffed the palms of my hands, which had so briefly touched his soft dark hair. I pressed them to my face. Then I tipped my head back, counted to ten.

I stole back inside, hoping no one had noticed. Ethan was nowhere to be seen.

"Oh—Tri, there you are," Aunt Tabby said from the kitchen. "Can you come in here for a moment?"

I glimpsed at Sydney and Su, then nodded and obeyed my aunt. But I stayed in the threshold area. I somehow felt they would be able to tell what had just happened in the entryway.

"Come, come to the table," Tabby said.

I shook my head. "I'll just stand," I said.

Tabby and Winter exchanged a glance.

Winter came right out with it. "Did you say there were new boys in school today?"

"Yes."

"What were they like?"

I looked at her a moment. "Just—boys," I said cautiously. "Teenage Alaska boys. Baseball caps. Blue jeans. Sweatshirts and flannel shirts."

"Where do they live?"

"They got on and off the bus about a mile from our stop."

"And you hadn't seen them before today?"

"No. No one had. Jack said they moved here from up the highway somewhere."

"And there are two of them?"

"Yes. Two. Wade and Jake James."

"Are they very young?"

"My age," I said. "Jake might be a little older. He's a senior. Why do you care?"

"Just curious," Winter said quickly. "And how was the rest of your day?"

"Okay."

"How's the arm?" Tabby asked.

"Okay."

They both smiled at me. What was it they weren't saying? What was it *everyone* wasn't saying?

I left the kitchen and went upstairs. I walked over to my window and sat down in my chair. "Oh brave new world," I whispered, remembering how Ms. Curtis once quoted Shakespeare in class, from *The Tempest*, "that has such people in it." I looked down at the guest cabin and searched for Ethan's pale face in the darkness of his window, but it was black and empty. Ethan. "Ethan," I whispered, just to hear the sound of his name. I tried to sort out his strange behavior in the entry and couldn't and returned, as I always did, to the moment in the woods: the wolf, then Ethan. The wolf.

Later that night, after Sydney and Tabby had left and the others had gone to bed, I glided down the stairs, my eyes taking in the familiar corners of the only home I'd ever known. It was so quiet and peaceful, the only sound the faint hiss of air pulling itself in through the damper on the wood stove. But I'd had a terrible thought, and I needed to check something. I took a step into the living room. Keats was there, curled by the fire, and I saw his eyes, bright and alert, find me in the dark. I turned on a light and walked quietly to the bookshelf. I knew what I was looking for, and my hand hesitated as it fluttered over my father's collection of books about wolves, though I knew exactly where it was. After a moment I let my hand touch the worn spine of the old book, but I didn't look at it as I removed it from its place and pulled a throw from the couch and joined Keats on the rug. Then I let myself see: *The Book of Were-Wolves: Being an Account of a Terrible Superstition* by Sabine Baring-Gould. I looked at the date on the title page: 1865. I scanned the introduction:

The traces left are indeed numerous enough, and though perhaps like the dodo or the dinornis, the werewolf may have become extinct in our age, yet he has left his stamp on classic antiquity, he has trodden deep in Northern snows, has ridden rough-shod over the medieavals, and has howled amongst Oriental sepulchers. . .

And then, another page: *What is Lycanthropy? The change of a man or a woman into the form of a wolf. . .so as to enable him or her to gratify the taste for human flesh, or through judgment of the gods in punishment for some great offense. . .*

I knew it was an accident, but Ethan *had* bitten me—hard. I put my hand over the still-sore spot and read until I couldn't keep my eyes open anymore. Then I turned off the light and fell asleep on the rug beside Keats, the words from the horrible book spinning in my mind—

His nails were long as claws, and were clotted with fresh gore, and shreds of human flesh . . .

☽

I heard breathing, and growling. Was I sleeping? I was dreaming of my room, but I didn't think I was there. Then I stood outside in Su's white nightgown, small on me with a fabric so thin. Ethan came up behind me and I felt his breath on the back of my neck, felt his nose in my hair. His arms circled my waist; I felt the length of him against the length of me. But where was the growling coming from? Was it him? And was someone calling my name?

I opened my eyes with a start and there was Ethan, silhouetted in the doorway, light behind him, looking at me through the dim dark of the room. Keats sat alert beside me, growling faintly. It was dark, but I could sense that it was morning, time to get up and get ready for school. Ethan looked at me and I looked at him and neither of us spoke.

The light from the hall fell across the floor, and his eyes found the book on the rug beside me. I moved quickly then, getting up, and I covered the book with the throw as I picked them both up. But as I stood and looked at him, I knew he knew somehow what I'd been reading. He held my gaze for a moment before taking a step backwards away from me. A wary step.

And the cautious look on his face brought home to me just why exactly I was reading the book in the first place, though it was a thought that seemed beyond the realm of the light of day.

Ten

All three of us went to school, Ethan walking amazingly well despite the wounds on his foot. He kept looking at me, though, darkly and quietly, and I wondered what he thought.

"Another day in history, Tri," Mr. Palmer said as we climbed the metal steps in a swirl of cold air and entered the bus.

I nodded and sat down. Ethan and Su sat behind me.

The book—that strange and awful book from my father's shelf—haunted me, though it seemed the author's intent was to prove that werewolves *didn't* exist: *Truly it consists in a form of madness, such as may be found in most asylums.* But then who would be mad? It seemed it would have to be me, since I was the one who might have seen what I kept thinking maybe I might have seen. Could it have been a dream? Could I just be imagining/exaggerating everything?

The James brothers were not at their stop. Mr. Palmer slowed the bus and looked down the road, but there was no sign of them. I breathed a sigh of relief. I looked out the dark window as Mr. Palmer re-closed the door and prepared to move the bus forward. But then someone from the back of the bus said, "Hey! Mr. Palmer! Wait! Here they come!" And I looked out the window in time to see Wade James sprinting alongside the bus and looking up at the row of windows, smiling. Smiling right at me.

"Boy, they're fast," I heard someone say as Mr. Palmer opened the door and the two rushed on board.

"I didn't see you two," Mr. Palmer said.

"Well, we were there," Jake James said, and the pair looked right at Ethan and Su as they walked toward an empty seat. Su smiled, but Ethan looked straight ahead, his jaw set tight.

I sat with Emma and Jack during lunch, not eating, giving monosyllabic answers to questions I could barely hear, my thoughts still engulfed with images of werewolves. (I reminded myself: the wolf I had seen in the woods with Ethan looked like a regular, ordinary wolf—not like those things in Sabine Baring-Gould's awful book.) Su sat nearby with her friends; Ethan was nowhere to be seen. And the James brothers were there, ever present, and I knew they were watching me. Why?

At one point Chris Evans walked by our table again; I wondered at it but couldn't bring myself to care. Then he looked straight at us and said, "Hello," and smiled as he passed on his way. Jack looked surprised, but I saw how Emma tried not to notice. I looked at her and she didn't look back.

A short time later, at my locker, I reorganized my books and pulled out what I needed for the next hour. Then I felt someone there.

"I'm Wade," he said. He leaned against the locker next to mine—Emma's locker—and I saw her frozen in the hall, watching.

I hesitated, then closed my locker and faced him.

"I don't bite," he said. His eyes were a blue so light they were almost white, not unlike Su's blue eye, not unlike the eyes of the huskies in Dangerous Dan's dog yard. His hair was thick and dark blond, unruly and unkempt. Again I smelled him: fresh air and clean water.

"Tri," I said.

"Try?"

"Tri. For Trileka."

"Oh. It's nice." Then I felt him start. His eyes moved across the surrounding area. I could feel Ethan nearby. And down the hall, a short distance away, Jake James.

Wade looked at me again. "It was nice to meet you," he said, and as he pulled away the air felt so thick I imagined I could almost see the separation of space between us.

Emma quickly took his place. Her mouth hung open. I shrugged casually, but I flashed on Ethan's strange words in the entry. With Emma by my side I headed out into the hall, aware of Wade James' loping stride behind me and Ethan's dark stare in front of me.

$$\mathcal{D}$$

At home, after dinner, Winter and I sat at the table. Winter knitted as she listened to a program on the radio; I pretended to do my homework. Su was in the living room reading a fashion magazine that came in the mail. Ethan was in the guest cabin.

"His foot healed awful fast," I said, not looking up. While he had been wincing that morning, when he reboarded the bus that afternoon you'd hardly know he'd been hurt.

"Hmm?"

I knew she'd heard me. "Ethan's foot. He didn't seem to have much of a problem walking today."

"Oh—that's good."

"It healed awful fast."

"So it did."

She continued her knitting. Eventually I went to bed.

I woke up sometime after midnight in the early hours. Su was in bed; I slipped into the bathroom for a moment then returned to the room. It was quiet; everything seemed okay. Su had tossed off her covers and I went to cover her back up. I took a sharp breath. She was naked. Her skin glowed in the dark of the room. I quickly covered her and darted to the window. I couldn't see anything. I stole hurriedly down the stairs and went out the back door. And there I could see it, somehow: Su's white nightgown on the white snowy ground not far from Ethan's guest cabin. I rushed out to it, picked it up and froze. There was strange breathing. I searched the darkness in front of me. Ethan was there; gradually I could see him, crouched in the cold. I took a tentative step toward him. He straightened and I could see that he wore no shirt; I could see the lean muscles of his chest and see how he glistened as if despite the temperature he was covered in sweat. I looked at the nightgown in my arms and looked at him. I think a small cry fell from my lips and he pounced forward. I leapt in through the back door and twisted the lock closed. He pressed against the window; I think he said my name. I plunged down the hall to the other door and locked that, too. Keats by now was awake and barking. Winter appeared on the stairs.

"Tri! What is it?"

"It's Ethan! He's out there! Su's nightgown!" I held up the nightgown as if that explained everything.

Winter rushed to me. "Shhh! Shhh! It's all right."

"It's not! It's not! Are you crazy? Am I crazy?"

"No—no, listen, Tri, listen to me—"

"No more lies! Don't you lie to me!"

"Ethan has an affliction. Su has it, too. It's in my family and yours.

76

But it's all right; they'll outgrow it. They're just going to act strange, some strange things will happen—"

"Su is *naked*, Winter—naked. She was outside and she was naked. With Ethan!"

"No, Tri, no, no, no. Ethan was helping her. That's all. That's all it would have been. That's all it would have been."

"Helping her? Helping her how?"

"Keeping her from—running off."

"Is she sleepwalking?"

"Something like that. She doesn't know what's going on. Really, Tri. Really."

I sat down on the floor. I could feel Ethan watching from the back door window; Winter walked over, cracked the door open a little, and talked to him quietly. Then she helped me to my feet and led me back to bed. Together we slipped Su's nightgown on over her head. Winter kissed my forehead, like she used to when I was little, whispered again that it was all right, and left the room, leaving the doors to both bedrooms open. I just lay there, shaking. Whatever was going on my sister had been naked, naked in front of Ethan. This seemed to bother me as much as anything.

In the morning I found I couldn't face them, any of them. Winter was up before me and made the coffee and packed the lunches. Ethan kept looking at me, but I couldn't look at him. Su acted like everything was normal. On the bus Mr. Palmer wanted to talk about history. I faked a smile and nodded.

"We're living it now," he said. "Living in history."

But I couldn't feel the connection, not today. I sat in my seat, my face leaning against the cold window, aware of Ethan and my sister sitting together in the seat behind me. Were they touching each other? Did he think about her naked body as he sat beside her?

When the James brothers got on, I felt Wade look at the empty seat beside me. Then I felt him look at Ethan, then Jake shoved him forward, and he went past. And so we went to school. We went to school and bells rang and classes stopped and started and Emma and Jack chattered about the upcoming homecoming dance and at some point I found myself alone in the hall, my forehead pressed against the cool hard surface of my locker door.

"You're not mad at me for some reason, are you, Tri?" Emma

appeared and looked at me, her forehead wrinkled in concern.

"Should I be?"

"No."

"What's with you and Chris Evans?"

"What?" But I felt, rather than saw, the look on her face.

I waited.

"Nothing," Emma said. "Nothing. Okay. He asked me to the dance. To homecoming."

"Are you going?"

"No! What kind of a friend do you think I am?"

"The kind that didn't tell me in the first place."

"Tri—"

"It's all right," I said. I had other things to think about. I told myself that. But I was aware of a lonely new feeling in my heart.

"I was going to, I just—"

"I know you want to go with him, Emma, so go."

"That's not true."

"I can *feel* it, okay?"

"Tri—"

"Emma, I don't care."

"Yes, you do."

"No."

"But something's wrong."

"Everything's wrong, Emma, right now—okay?"

She took a step back. "What's wrong? Tri, you can tell me. What is it?"

I shook my head. I couldn't tell her.

Eleven

I couldn't eat; I couldn't sleep. I avoided everyone. Somehow the rest of the week went by, one day after another. Wolves killed another of Dan's dogs. From my room I could see Ethan pacing in the night; sometimes Winter joined him, sometimes when he wasn't there Winter dashed off into the woods, disappearing for hours. Sometimes he was there in the window, looking up at me.

Su grew more sullen. The snow fell. And Wade James said hello to me each and every day in the halls of River Valley High—his brother, my sister, and Ethan all looking on, three sets of hostile eyes.

And then I saw it. And then I knew.

It was Saturday, cold and gray. I walked Keats in the woods. If there were wolves around I didn't care. I simply had to get out of the house, though I did grab my father's shotgun, just in case. Then Keats stopped and froze. I thought, *Wolves.* But I looked through the trees and saw Ethan. He looked so alone, so very alone. And he looked beautiful—slim and graceful, his hair long and loose around his pale face. I felt a longing for him, and then I remembered: he had seen my sister naked. They had been together, and she had been naked.

Suddenly he began to shake, so violently I could see it even at a distance. Then he fell onto his knees, then he curled up into a ball. He tossed and turned on the ground. Then Ethan was gone and in his place there was a wolf—white and silver with bits of black—shaking itself free of Ethan's clothing before it ran off into the trees.

I saw it. I did. And that's what I told Winter.

"That's his affliction, as you call it, that's it, isn't it?" I said. She was in the kitchen at the table. Su, thankfully, was visiting a friend. "He turns into a wolf. He is a wolf. A werewolf. A monster. Like out of the movies. Like in that book of Dad's. Only it's true!"

"Tri—"

"And you said Su is the same. Su my sister. She's a wolf. A wolf person."

"Tri—please—" She guided me into a chair, the shotgun still strapped across my chest.

"How long does it last?"

"It doesn't go away, Tri, but it does get better. The teen years are the worst."

"Is Su—has Su—"

She hesitated. Not for long but long enough for me to catch it. "No—not that I know of," she said. "But it's starting."

"What about the wolves? The wolves in the yard?"

"They're not here to hurt anyone."

I remembered my father's words. "Don't tell me—don't tell me. They're here because they like us, right?"

She searched my face. "Something like that. But it's—it's not that simple. They want us—well, in this case Ethan and Su—they want them back."

"Back?"

Winter nodded. "That part of us. . .belongs to them. The pack. To them, we're their family, and they want us back. And they can get us back, when we're vulnerable like Ethan and Su. We can turn—forever."

"Oh." I didn't like those words.

"We're not werewolves, Tri."

"What's the difference?"

"We don't kill people, for one thing!"

"When were you ever going to tell me?"

"Soon. Soon. Oh, Tri. It's not an easy thing to tell anyone."

"Why does Su have it?"

"Because your father had it."

"Daddy? No—. He couldn't have been a wolf! What about my mother? Did she have it? How come I don't have it?"

"You don't have it because your mother didn't have it, Tri—though you do have a genetic memory that shows itself in your dreams and sometimes your senses are heightened. But Ethan bit you. That could—that could give it to you, but I'm hoping not. Your father was so happy that you were free. You were free. He was so happy about that."

I almost actually laughed. I had always thought of myself as the most un-free person I knew: there were always things that needed to be taken care of, and I always ended up doing them. Then something dawned on me, like a black cloud rising in front of my face. "Did my mother know?"

"Not at first."

"And then she found out, didn't she?"

Winter nodded.

"And then she left."

Winter nodded again. And so something that had long been a mystery was made clear. She left because she didn't want us. She didn't want us because we were monsters.

"Tabby?" I asked. "Is she—?"

Winter nodded, then added, "Not Sydney, but he knows."

"So everyone knows," I said. "Everyone except me and Su."

That night I sat in the dark of my room by my window, looking out at the night with its circle of moon peeking in and out of the cloud layer, waiting for morning to come. I was not going to go to sleep. I would not sleep because if I did, I might wake up thinking everything was okay, and then I would have to go through it all again, play it through my brain, registering, remembering, knowing.

Things were not the same. Things would never be the same again.

I remembered this feeling from when my dad died—or disappeared. I remembered sitting here, at this very window, fighting sleep so I wouldn't have to wake, so I wouldn't have to have those few brief moments of normalcy before reliving everything all over again. It was easier to stay in the pain.

After a while I slipped out to the bathroom. I brushed my teeth in the darkness, watching the ghostly reflection of my face in the mirror. *It's all right,* I told myself, trying out the words, letting them circle the edges of my emotions. When my mother left, didn't everyone tell me and Su it would be all right? I felt like I could remember that, the repetition of those words. And had it been all right? Su and I had survived, but there was always this weight—a gray cloud-like weight— hanging there. But there was a lot of happiness, too, which came in time: Christmases, school plays, sledding with our dad, then my dad and Winter's happy summer wedding with Su and me the flower girls and all the wild roses blooming everywhere. And then, of course, our dad died. We got used to that, eventually, like we got used to our mother being gone. As I looked at my pale face in the dark mirror, wondering what any of it meant, I realized I had to do now what I had always done: Be there for Su. Help her get through it—through this strange and terrible thing—and in that way help myself make it, too. It was the only thing that I could do.

$$\smallsmile$$

"Let us see it, Tri."

Winter and Tabby hovered over me as I sat at the kitchen table. "It's fine," I said. It was Sunday evening, nine days since Ethan had bit me and just over twenty-four hours since I'd seen what I'd seen.

"Please," Winter said. "Just humor us."

Humor us. I felt myself smirk. Who'd been the one humored around here—for her entire life? I pulled up the sleeve of the gray sweatshirt Wade James had left on the bus Friday. He'd dropped it on the way out and Mr. Palmer had tossed it back into the empty half of my seat. When I left, I'd swooped it up with my stuff. No one saw me but when I slipped into the car all three of them—Ethan, Su, Winter—were acting like something smelled—looking, sniffing. I didn't think much of it then. But now I knew better. And I also knew there was something about Wade James the wolves in my family didn't like.

I didn't know why I was wearing the sweatshirt, only that it was like having a secret.

Winter and Tabby's long fingers gently ran over the surface of my forearm. There were fresh pink scars, and the skin there felt warmer than elsewhere on my body, but it wasn't unpleasant. I knew, right there above my head, Winter and Tabby were talking to each other with their eyes. Now that I had finally noticed this I realized how often they did it—a secret language long practiced, words without sound.

"How are you feeling these days, Tri?" Tabby asked. Both she and Winter had been circling around me all day.

"Just fine," I said flatly. What could I say? How was I supposed to be feeling?

"Tri," Tabby had said earlier, following me out to the woodshed. "Tri—this is something I never wanted to be. This isn't a choice. Look at me, Tri."

Reluctantly I'd lifted my eyes, my arms half-loaded with wood. Ethan had been splitting it—big stacks, the pieces thinner than they needed to be. And I didn't even need to be out there; Ethan had brought in the wood (and he'd shoveled the drive, and he'd even washed the dishes). But I couldn't stand being in the house, with Tabby and Winter watching me and with Su being all blessedly oblivious.

"I know how you feel, Tri, because once I felt the exact same thing."

I'd looked away but stayed still.

"I was young once too, you know. I was young and wanted things to only be normal—I wanted only to be normal. Like the other kids. Winter, too—she went through this, too. It's not a choice. It's something we have to bear. Not something we want."

I couldn't answer. I had nothing to say.

"It will get better," Tabby had continued. "It will. People get through all kinds of things in this world, Tri. Our situation is just a little more unusual, that's all. But it will get better."

Now Winter said, "You know we're concerned about Ethan's bite."

I pulled my arm away from their flurrying fingers. "Maybe Ethan's bark," I said, "is bigger than his bite."

More silent words. I probably nearly knocked both their chins with the top of my head as I rose from the table just as the phone rang.

"Hello?" I said, picking up the phone and ignoring Winter's attempt to beat me to it.

"Yes—is this the Blue Moon Bed and Breakfast?" a woman's voice asked. She had some kind of an accent—German, maybe.

"Yes, it is," I said. "One moment please." I handed the phone to Winter and left the kitchen. In the foyer, Su sat at the bottom of the stairs.

"He likes you and you ignore him," she growled.

I looked at my little sister and felt a twisting on my heart. Did she realize anything that was happening to her?

"It's like you made him like you so he wouldn't like me. And now you just ignore him. And you wear *his* smelly sweatshirt."

"Su," I said. "That's not how it is."

"Oh? Then how is it?"

I felt her anger, on the verge of spilling over. I thought of all the things I had done for her, year after year after year, but bit my tongue. I was still the big sister. I needed to always remember that. Somehow, I needed to help her.

"I don't know how it is," I said softly. "But I don't think you have to worry about Ethan liking me."

"He hates Wade James. You can tell that. And that's because Wade likes you. And you're always talking to Wade in the hall.'"

"He says hi to me, Su. I'm not sure that constitutes 'like.'"

Su let a puff of air vibrate out between her lips. "You just want all the new boys," she snarled then slunk away up the stairs.

"Tri," Winter said, suddenly emerging from the kitchen. "We've got guests coming this week. They're bringing a dog team. They're from Merlin River, and there's not much snow there yet this year, so they're going to stay a whole week."

I looked at her. Normally this would be good news—in terms of the money, which with Christmas coming and next summer far off I knew we needed. But—. "Do they know about the wolves?" I snapped. I meant the ones that were killing Dan's dogs—not the ones living in my house.

Winter's eyes grew round. "No—and we're not telling them."

"Don't you think we should?"

"Tri—we need this money. And the wolves haven't been back around *here*. We'll keep an eye out, and an ear out, and trust me if they come around we'll know, and then we'll get out your dad's shotgun and take care of it. But I don't think they'll come around again. We— we're quite a group now."

"Hmm," I said. I knew what she was saying. We were a pack of our own.

In the morning, Wade's sweatshirt seemed to have disappeared. I slammed the door as I left the house and stood outside in the dark while the car warmed. After a few minutes I watched them emerge from the entryway: Su, Ethan, Winter. Wolves.

In school Emma and Jack followed me hopelessly around. One thing I knew: I couldn't tell them. I couldn't tell anybody. Emma still thought that I was angry over Chris Evans; she kept saying, "I don't care about him, Tri, really" and refused to believe that it really wasn't about him.

Gradually Emma and Jack quit trying though they stayed by my side, and in the end I was grateful for their quiet companionship. At one point in the day, after they went on to gym class ahead of me and I was still in the hall, I let myself have a moment alone by my locker, and I felt hot tears sting my eyes.

Everything seemed out of my reach now—everything I had always dreamed of. What kind of a life could I have, if my sister was a wolf? Who would ever want to go out with me, knowing the truth about my family? How could I go off to college and leave Su on her own? I stared at the cold blue metal in front of me, suddenly too tired to move.

"Hey."

The voice startled me. I turned and there was Wade James. We just looked at each other for a minute, and I felt my eyes well up with tears.

"I'm your friend," he said quietly.

Somehow it seemed like he was. Somehow. *How do you know me?* I wanted to say. *How?* But my lips failed to move.

"Remember that, okay?"

I nodded, and he touched a tear that fell down my cheek. Then he walked away, looking back to see me watching him go.

Two short days. Two short days later I would be whisked away from those halls, from those benign chatterings, from history: I would not know that Mr. Palmer and Jack and Emma would all call my house, concerned because Su and I stopped showing up for the bus, stopped showing up for school; I would not know that even Chris Evans would ask where I was—where we all were: me, Su, Ethan. . .and Wade and Jake James.

Twelve

That Tuesday, after school, I glumly helped Winter get the second—and largest—guest cabin ready. The clients would be arriving after dark, and we hooked up some extra outside lights so they would be able to see where they could fix their dogs. This cabin was the best one, I'd always thought, with a round window in the gable at one end and a fairy-tale loft bedroom with a moon and stars and winter trees painted on the walls and ceiling. We called it the Moonflower.

"I'm going to move Ethan into the house," Winter said as we snapped a patchwork quilt into place on the bed. "I think I'll put him in my room, and I'll sleep downstairs. Just in case." Together we turned the top of the quilt down so some lace from the sheet showed.

"In case of what?"

"Oh—I guess in case of wolves. Or something."

"Su will think that's weird," I said flatly, fluffing a pillow. What I really wanted to say was, should they be sleeping that close to each other? I knew sleeping wasn't something I'd be doing, what with him right across the hall. But I knew I needed sleep. I needed sleep so I could think. My head was so tired.

"I'll just say it's because of his foot," Winter said. Ethan's foot, which had initially healed so quickly, was now swollen and possibly infected. But what could he expect, I thought, running around in the woods every night and refusing to stay home from school?

"Tri," Winter began, touching me lightly as I turned toward the door. I felt my skin crawl as I knew something was coming. "Tri, you need to be—careful. Around those new boys. Okay? Don't go anywhere with them."

I looked at her, my eyes narrow and suspicious. "Why?"

"It's. . .complicated."

I snorted. "More complicated than what you've already told me?" That seemed pretty impossible. "Is Ethan going to bite them if he thinks they like me?"

"No—no, Tri."

"Then why?"

She shook her head.

"If you don't tell me, I'll do whatever with them."

"All right. Our—" She hesitated.

"Affliction." I said, not without sarcasm. Affliction was much too mild a word.

"There's a mutant strain of it. There are others."

"Others?"

She nodded. "Others like us but not. They're dangerous, Tri."

"You mean, like werewolves instead of just wolf-people?" I knew I sounded glib but I didn't care.

"Yes. You could it put it like that."

I thought again of my father's book. Wouldn't Sabine Baring-Gould love to know me. Or not. But Wade—a werewolf? "Wade and—" I began, but then I thought of Jake, lurking in the hall, staring. And of course, I remembered Ethan's strange words in the entry. "Wade is nice," I said quietly. How could he possibly be something awful? I felt tears and squashed them down. Everywhere I turned I felt like I was running into a dark corner.

"And he might be. We just don't know. Give us a little time to figure it out."

"Us?"

"Well, Ethan, Tabby, and me. We should be able to sort it out soon."

"Did you take his sweatshirt?"

Winter nodded.

"There's something. . .about them that you smell."

She nodded again.

"So they're not normal."

She shook her head. "But it could be that they're only like us."

"Or they could be the others."

And she nodded again.

Later, when the guests came, I noticed the dogs right away. I noticed something wasn't quite right, but I couldn't put my finger on it. I was out in the dark and the cold, helping the guests unload the huskies from the back of their big shiny black pick-up where a custom-made camper-top housed individual kennels lined with hay. I suddenly realized something, something I had never thought about before. That when we had guests with dogs, I was the one who helped; Winter was always otherwise occupied. Because I wasn't a carrier of the so-called family "affliction," and the dogs wouldn't be afraid of me.

These dogs were white Siberian huskies. Every one of them, white. They stared at me with complacent eyes but followed obediently as I gently tugged at their chains so I could lead them to where their master was laying out a temporary dog yard, spreading out beds of hay on the snow. The dogs were white, gentle, and very, very quiet. Their master—Dr. Hanns—was tall, broad, dark eyed, dark bearded and, like his dogs, quiet. I handed him the ends of the chains I was holding. "These are the last two," I said.

His dark eyes slid into their corners, looking at me. "Thank you," he said, his voice low.

"Can I do anything else for you?" I asked.

His mouth cracked into a slight smile which creased his angular cheeks. "No, but thank you."

"Let us know if you need anything," I said, suddenly wanting to be out of there. I took a step backwards and turned around. The man's wife appeared in front of me, wearing a very tight looking black snow suit. She had beautiful blond hair that cascaded across her shoulders.

"It's very lovely," she said in the accent I still figured was German. "We will be comfortable. We will tell you of our needs."

I felt I was being dismissed and was more than happy to be so. I gave her a nod and stepped around her, noticing that she, too, took steps to widen the distance between us as I passed. I hurried into the house, where an unhappy Keats was sequestered inside so the dog team wouldn't act up at the sight of him. I petted his big head and let him smell all the new scents on me. Then all at once he started barking—at me! I took a step back. "Keats! Stop it!" I said. His bark was deafeningly loud inside the house. Ethan and Su appeared at the top of the stairs, looking down at me. Then Winter emerged from the kitchen.

"Keats!" she said, kneeling down beside him and laying her arm across his bristling back. "Keats—stop it now, hush. It's okay. Yes, there are other dogs out there and yes, Tri has handled them. But hush. . .it's okay." And Keats quieted but he looked at me strangely, almost pleadingly, before sulking away to his spot by the wood stove in the living room.

I saw something on Winter's face. A flash of concern. She followed Keats to the living room, turned off the light and walked over to a dark window. I knew what she was looking at and felt a chill: the Moonflower, where our new—and interesting—guests were staying. A few moments later she drew the cotton curtains closed, walked past me and through the entryway where I heard her locking the door. Then she walked past me again, went upstairs, and brought down an armful of bedding from her room where Ethan would now be staying. She put these on the couch in the living room, then approached me and talked quietly, almost in a whisper. "Tri," she said. "I don't want you to worry. But I want you to take your father's shotgun upstairs to your room with you tonight. Keep it close."

"What is it? What's wrong?"

She shook her head. "It's probably nothing. It's been. . .a very stressful few weeks. I know you know that. I haven't been immune to that, either, Tri."

I met her brown-black eyes. I could suddenly see how tired she was.

"It's probably nothing," she said again. But she waited in the threshold of the living room until I finished shutting down the house and took my father's shotgun down from the kitchen wall and up the stairs with me.

The door to Winter's room was slightly cracked. I felt Ethan's dark eyes on me as I opened the door to my own room, the gun heavy in my hand. I leaned the gun into a corner near my bed. I left the lights off—Su slept already—and found my pajamas in the dark, pulled them on then looked carefully out my window. Nothing moved—the night seemed still, quiet, at peace. I thought again how very quiet the visiting dog team was and I realized that *that* was what didn't seem right to me when I was helping Dr. Hanns tie them up in the make-shift dog yard: there wasn't a bark, or a whine, or a yelp from any of the thirteen dogs—just a squeezy breathing sound as if they were being choked. But the collars on the dogs I'd handled seemed fine—not too loose, not too tight. I resolved to find out more about them in the morning.

I climbed into the cool covers on my bed and lay on my back listening to the night as my body warmed the sheets and blankets. I told myself quiet was good—no howling, no barking, no need to wonder if something was out there. I thought about Ethan in the next room and wondered if he slept. I thought not. I thought I wouldn't sleep, either, that night, but before I knew it, I was lost in a dream, and that dream was about Wade James.

There was snow and cold, and his face was close to mine. I felt a yearning from deep down inside of me. But then I saw Ethan, half lost in a swirl of snow over Wade's shoulder, and the yearning turned into a longing, a break-your-heart longing, and I reached past Wade's broad shoulder toward Ethan, but he was receding into the snow, vanishing—

Then I woke up and heard a strange sound. It sounded like someone crying, or someone trying to cry out through a mouth stuffed with rags. In the bed next to me Su still slept; I whispered a quick quiet thanks, grabbed my father's gun and slipped out of my room and down the stairs, unsure of where the noise was coming from.

Winter was awake and stood looking out one of the windows, toward the Moonflower. She kept the lights off and the room was dark.

"They can't bark," she said in a whisper as I approached.

I looked out the window with her. Our two guests were up and about, dressed in their tight slick snow gear, hooking up their white dogs to their sled. "What do you mean?" I asked. I could see how the dogs' mouths moved yet offered little sound.

"They must have taken out their voice boxes," Winter said.

"What?"

"Some people do that, Tri. If they have a lot of dogs like this but live in a place where they have to watch the noise. It keeps the neighbors happy. But what a sound. . .what a sound."

It was truly mournful, a sound like a smothered scream. I shook my head and felt a tightening in my throat. "How can they do that? How could they do that to those dogs?"

"I don't know," she said. We watched as the man turned from the team and took several strides toward the house. "He's coming. Go meet him. Go see what he wants, Tri—now—please."

There was an urgency in her voice I could not argue with, despite the fact that I was still in my pajamas and hadn't even gone to the bathroom yet. I put down the gun and grabbed my coat, aware of Keats' silent stare as I hurried to the door.

I met Dr. Hanns halfway to the guest cabin. He stopped and surveyed me, tipping his head then looking toward the window where Winter, I was sure, still watched. Then he looked at me and waited. I didn't know what I was supposed to say, and a long awkward moment passed.

"Yes?" he said. "You want something?"

"No—I. . .was just coming to see if there's anything you need."

"No," he said. "I was only going to see if you had an outdoor thermometer."

"Yes," I said. "But there's also one over there." I nodded toward the Moonflower. "It's on a birch tree, out front."

"Thank you." He smiled and I saw the glint of his white teeth. "But tell me, are you the special one of the house?" His eyes gleamed as he looked down at me.

I didn't know what he meant. "Special?"

"Special. The treasure. The one who is different from the rest."

"No," I said. "I'm not special. What makes you think that?"

"You seem to be the household ambassador," he replied. "But no matter. You have a nice day, miss Trileka." He turned.

"Do you know where the trails are?" I asked hurriedly.

"I don't need any trails," he said.

I looked toward the woods where Keats and I, just a few short weeks ago, had rescued Ethan from Dan's trap. The cries of the silenced white huskies filled my ears. "Just don't go that way," I said, pointing. "There are wolf traps."

He looked over his shoulder, his dark brows raised in mild curiosity. "Which way?"

"That way," I pointed again.

"Wolf traps," he said, turning again, and I swore I could hear him laugh.

☽

After getting home from school that day I had to get out of and away from the house, and though Winter protested and Keats refused to come, I finally did so shortly before the daylight began to leave us once again. It was cold, and I dressed warmly: down jacket, fleece pants, Sorrels. Winter insisted I take the shotgun, which I did, and I felt Ethan's eyes on me as I hurried out the door and into the fresh cold air.

I walked down the road a ways to where a trail cut off toward a nearby ridge. A snowmachine had recently traveled down it, packing the snow for good walking, and I could also see evidence of the recreational habits of local skiers. But in the woods I saw no one, and it was blessedly peaceful and quiet. The gun felt heavy on my shoulder, and I tried not to think about anything but the clean cold air and the sound of chickadees singing in the trees. I was almost able to relax when I rounded a bend where the trail came out on the edge of one of the many ridges in the neighborhood and saw right in front of me the object of my past night's dream: Wade James. And nearby, as always, lurked his brother Jake.

Wade was sitting on a snowmachine looking at something through a pair of binoculars; Jake was crouched in the snow, looking in the same direction. They both saw me, but neither seemed surprised. Wade motioned with his hand for me to approach where he sat; I hesitated. It wasn't just Winter's words. I had slipped Wade's sweatshirt, after Winter gave it back to me, into the lost and found and I saw him retrieve it. He put it right to his nose. Then instantly he looked across the student center, straight at me.

He looked straight at me again now as he saw me thinking. Winter had to be wrong, I reasoned. Not everybody could be a freak. And I had a gun. I walked over to him and he handed me his binoculars. I took a look. Down past the bottom of the ridge in a difficult looking snow-filled gully I could see our guests maneuvering nimbly with their dog team, each standing on a runner at the back of the sled.

"They're our guests," I said, handing the binoculars back to Wade. "They came here to run their dogs."

There was something on Wade's face, but I couldn't read it. Like he wanted to know something. "They've never stayed with us before," I offered. "They're from Merlin River. They've had their dogs' voice boxes removed."

"A hennas practice," Jake snapped, rising from his crouching position. He took a step toward Wade. "Let's go," he said. Instinctively I stepped back and out of the way. With a quick pull Jake started his machine and swung onto it in front of Wade. "You should go home, Tri," Wade said, his voice strangely audible above the growl of the machine. After a quick turn around, they were gone. I listened for a few moments as the noise of the machine disappeared into the woods. Then silence fell, and I felt a chill. I knew at once why. In the woods around me there were wolves.

Quickly I got the shotgun loaded and pumped. I held it low in my hands and swung it side to side as I walked backwards down the trail. The wolves hung back in the woods, but I could see them—glimpses of them, slinking between the trees. The sound of my heart was a rhythmic crashing in my ears, and my breath shot out in rapid frosty bursts. But as I walked, one backwards step at a time, I began to realize how alert I was, how awake I was, and how powerful I was with my father's gun ready in my capable hands. These wolves would not get me—and then at once I realized they didn't even *want* to get me. I felt myself straighten. The wolves seemed farther behind now. I took a deep breath and turned around and nearly walked straight into Wade James.

"They don't want to hurt you," he said, looking past me into the woods.

"I think I know that," I said. "Generally, wolves don't hurt people."

But something shifted on his face, and he concentrated on the woods behind us. I looked over my shoulder and saw several of the wolves—running right toward us on the trail—and before I could even react, they leapt off the trail and continued running off into the woods.

"They're coming," Wade said.

"Who?"

"The dog team." He looked ahead of us and raised his hand, signaling to Jake who I could just glimpse through the trees. Then all at once he lifted me up off my feet and swung me a good yard off the trail, leaping the distance after me. He grabbed my free hand and pulled me back into the trees, stopping behind a cluster of thick white birch.

"What's wro—" I began, but Wade quickly covered my mouth with his mittened hand. A fearful thought then flashed in my mind: Winter and Ethan were suspicious of Wade and Jake. Had they just captured me? But as he held his hand over my mouth with my head pressed back against a tree and his body almost pressed against mine, I felt like I could trust him—that like the wolves in the woods, he was not here to hurt me.

I heard the dog team coming on the trail, heard the hiss of the runners and the muffled trampling of the dogs' paws. I listened as they sped past where we hid, and they were a good way down the trail before Wade took his hand off my mouth.

"What's that all about?" I asked, whispering.

He shook his head. "You don't want to know."

"Do you know them?"

He looked at me. "Just stay away from them, Tri."

"Well I can't exactly do that," I said. "They're our guests."

"How long are they staying?"

"A week."

"Hmm."

"So do *you* know them?" I asked again, but he wouldn't answer. I began taking the shells out of the chamber of the shotgun, but Wade said, "Just keep the safety on. You're not home yet." He walked back to the trail and motioned for me to follow. The woods were quiet, eerie. And it was getting dark.

Jake was waiting with the snowmachine where the trail crossed the road. When he saw us, he started it and hopped on, and Wade motioned for me to get on behind Jake.

"I can walk," I said.

"It'll be getting dark soon," Wade said.

"I can handle it," I said.

"No," he said. "Let us take you home." He firmly but gently pulled the gun out of my hand and nudged me toward the machine. I shook my head and took a step back.

"Tri," he began, but just then the headlights of Dangerous Dan's truck appeared, and I snatched my shotgun back and lifted my hand so Dan would stop, immediately regretting my decision but at the same time I just wasn't ready to put all my faith in my earlier feeling that I could trust Wade. I knew Dan.

"Hello Trileka," Dan said as he leaned across his front seat toward the passenger side window which he'd opened. "Everything all right?"

"Yes," I said quickly. "But I was wondering if you could drop me off at home. We just saw some wolves."

That was all I needed to say. Dan nodded vigorously and pushed open the door. "You boys want a ride somewhere, too?"

Wade and Jake each shook their head.

"Well watch yourselves now. You'll probably be all right on that machine, but I'd get home if I were you."

Wade nodded but kept his eyes on me. He looked like he wanted to say something but didn't.

"So how many?" Dan asked as he shifted the old truck into gear.

"What?" I had the strangest feeling as we pulled away and Wade's eyes stayed on mine. A feeling of regret and apprehension.

"Wolves. How many were there?"

"I only saw three or four. But I think there were more."

I could see his jaw clench. "Back there on the ridge trail?"

"Yes."

"I wish it wasn't getting dark," he said. "If it wasn't, I'd go after them." He glanced down at my gun. "Glad to see you're protecting yourself, Tri."

I didn't respond, and he dropped me off in front of my house and waited until I was safely in the doorway. I turned and waved, feeling strangely tender toward Dan as I watched his red taillights disappear down the drive. It *was* getting dark now, and a full moon was coming up through the trees. And I was a second away from walking straight into a nightmare.

Thirteen

I hadn't noticed that there were no lights on in the house when Dan and I had pulled into the drive; if I had, I might have known something was not right before I crossed through the entryway and opened the door to the inside. As my eyes adjusted to the dim afternoon light, the first thing I saw was Keats, dead or unconscious I didn't know, lying at the foot of the stairs in a dark puddle.

Then I heard, from the kitchen, a sound not unlike that of the voiceless huskies—a straining, strangled, gasping sound. It all happened very fast—in a second. I swung my father's gun off my shoulder, flicked off the safety and raised the sights to my eyes as I moved to the kitchen where a dark struggling mass was against the wall. I tipped my elbow up and turned on the light. I shot. Just like that. And the man who was strangling Winter—killing Winter with big, hairy hands—crumbled to the floor. Winter, too, collapsed.

"Run!" Winter gasped. I could see she was bruised and bloody. There were streaks of blood on the wall where she had been pinned.

"Where's Su? Where's Su!"

"They've got her! Just run, Tri, run! Go!"

I heard a cry from out back.

Winter shook her head. "Listen, Tri. Listen! This man isn't dead. This man isn't a man. Listen to me! You can't stop them with a gun. You have to get out of here!"

"No! Su!" I ran to the back door and burst outside. Over by the dog team the woman—Mrs. Hanns—struggled with Su.

"Su! Get down!" I yelled, lifting the shotgun. But they continued to move, and I couldn't see clear. As I rushed toward them my foot caught something warm and yielding. I looked down and oh, my heart broke and stopped—

Ethan lay still, covered in blood.

Su screamed.

I rushed forward. Instead of shooting I lifted the rifle and brought the stock down hard on the woman's head. She wavered, then fell with a groan. And to my shock Su was gone and a sleek black wolf with white markings gripped the woman's leg, blood oozing from Mrs. Hann's snowmachine suit. Then I saw all around a scrambled pile of clothes. Su's clothes. "Oh no, oh no, oh no!" I said. "Su! *Su!*"

The wolf looked up at me with a bloody mouth, then fled into the dark woods.

"Su!" I yelled but she was gone.

The woman at my feet groaned. Rope. I needed rope. I needed Winter. I ran toward the house. I knelt quickly by Ethan, touched him. Was he dead? I thought of the phone and rushed inside to the kitchen.

It was empty. There was blood on the floor where Winter had been, blood pooled on the floor where Dr. Hanns had fallen. And two bloody trails leaving the kitchen.

I groped for light switches, looked down at the trails. They both went toward the door. Winter was crawling, I could tell that. Bloody handprints. And then the handprints turned to wolf prints. Her clothes lay scattered.

I grabbed the phone receiver and started punching numbers. Dan. He was closest. The troopers were fifteen miles away. And Tabby and Sydney had gone to town.

The phone rang and rang. "Yello," the answering machine said. "This is Dan. I'm probably just out in the dog yard, so say your piece, and I'll get back to you."

"It's Trileka! We need help!"

Then I heard something in the entryway. I put the receiver back in the cradle. In a drawer just below the phone were the extra boxes of shotgun shells. I grabbed handfuls and shoved them into the pockets of my coat.

Then Dr. Hanns appeared in the threshold of the kitchen. But it wasn't Dr. Hanns. His face was changing before my eyes—teeth, jaws, fur, claws—all appeared out of nowhere and he stayed bipedal and growled and snapped his mouth as he came toward me.

I raised the shotgun and pumped and shot, pumped and shot. It slowed him but didn't stop him. I heard what sounded like a snowmachine outside, and I prayed to God it wasn't Dan, I prayed to God he wouldn't come *now* and get himself killed.

Then I heard glass breaking behind me.

"Tri! Hurry!"

Wade James appeared in a broken window. "Now!"

I fired again and fell backwards into Wade's arms as he grabbed me and pulled me out the window. We leapt onto the snowmachine behind Jake and sped away, the monster that was Dr. Hanns rushing out the window after us as we left, and his wife now, appearing from the side, face distorted and canine, taking a desperate leap at us.

We rushed forward into growing darkness, zooming past trees and plunging down ridges. After about a half hour we stopped and from a thicket of brush the brothers pulled out a loaded sled and hooked it to their machine.

"Who are you?" I asked.

Wade shook his head. "We have to keep moving. We have to keep going." And he and Jake climbed back on the machine, and we zoomed off again. As I rode—wedged in between the two of them—I tried to put my mind back together. Su was alive, I told myself. Out there somewhere as a wolf but alive. Ethan might be dead. And Keats. And Winter, too. Did the monsters stay, to finish things off? To kill Dan when he came? Or were they running after us right now. Or were they running after Su.

I tried to twist my head around so Wade would hear me. "Su," I said.

"She'll have to keep going," Wade said. "Her instincts will kick in, and if she lets them, the other wolves will help her."

"Ethan," I choked.

I felt Wade tremble. "We had to choose," he said. "Him or you. I chose you."

We continued on, only stopping to refuel the snowmachine from a jug of gas on the sled. I didn't know for sure, but I felt we were heading for the mountains, for the high country. "When the moon sets, or when we can see far, we can stop," Wade said. "But not before."

I looked at the moon then, a once beloved celestial entity. Now it seemed it was my enemy. The moon and the night.

$$\smallsmile$$

It was morning of the next day before we stopped for more than a few minutes. We stood on the top of a lonely ridge. Wade and Jake checked their watches, waited a few more minutes, checked again, then proceeded to set up a quick camp.

"We need to sleep," Wade said. "It's safe now, for a while."

"How do you know?"

"Listen."

I listened. I heard an owl, somewhere in the valley below the ridge. I heard a wolf howl. I looked at Wade.

"It's all right," he said. "The moon's gone down and there would be nothing—no sound—if the weren were near."

"The what?"

"The weren. Werewolves. What you saw."

"Who are you?"

"I know you have questions, Tri. But now we need to sleep. Let's just say that we're—we're the same as your family. And we know of Ethan. We came here to help him."

"Know what of Ethan?"

"He's special. To our kind."

"But you left him."

Wade looked away. "We had to choose," he said softly. "We could smell him, but we couldn't find him. His blood was all over. And you were a second from death—or worse." He took a slow breath. "We couldn't stay. We all would have died. And we knew you were still alive." He paused, then added, very quietly, "I couldn't let you die."

"We have to go back," I said.

"We have to rest, then decide what to do."

I held back tears. I couldn't start crying now. I wouldn't stop. "I have to pee," I said, too tired and distraught to care that I was saying this to a boy I hardly knew. It all seemed a dream, and I hoped that I would sleep and wake to a different world.

"Go over there," he said, pointing to a cluster of scrubby spruce. "We'll watch."

"You'll what?"

He cracked a tired smile. "We'll watch the area," he clarified. "Not you."

"All right," I said wearily, handing him my shotgun to hold. I trudged through the snow to the trees. How could this be real? How could I explain it if it was?

A few minutes later I was wedged in a sleeping bag with Wade. Jake was in a separate bag on the other side of me. I could feel my body tingle with the nearness of Wade. There was nothing I could do about it. I closed my eyes and said prayers for Ethan, Su, Winter, and Keats and fell into a dark, dreamless sleep.

When I awoke it was still light, and I was alone in the tent. It took me a moment to remember where I was and why. That it was real felt like a slab of concrete crushing my soul. Then fear and worry and grief laid their heavy hands on my heart, and I could barely breathe. Where was Su? Had Winter survived? Ethan? And Keats, dear, dear Keats, Keats who I knew was trying to protect those I loved. I wondered what Dangerous Dan found, after he got my message, and if he still lived. Where Tabby and Sydney were, and if they knew. I had to find out. I had to find out these things. I took some deep breaths and crawled out of the tent, pulling on my boots which were all I had taken off before going to sleep. The day was glaringly bright and cold. I surveyed my surroundings, which I had been too tired to notice earlier. We were on a wide ridge. In back of us more hills and ridges rose, while in front of us a sweeping view spread out: hills and valleys and, far away, a frozen river. We were in the foothills of the mountains where my father's plane had disappeared, the ones we could see from our house on a clear day. I wondered how many miles we had traveled.

Wade and Jake sat by a small camp stove nearby. They watched me as I walked toward them. I knelt by the blue flame and spread my hands out toward the heat.

"What do we do now?" I asked.

"The moon is close enough to full again tonight," Wade said. "It could be very dangerous for us, if they're hunting us. If they're hunting the others, it will be dangerous for them."

"We need to find out what happened to everyone," I said.

"We need to stay alive," Jake said.

"So you said they're werewolves," I said.

"That's the common name for them," Wade said. "But we've never called them that. They're not wolves—at all. Not to us."

"What do they want with us—what do they want with my family?"

"They want Ethan," Wade said. "He's been hunted for some time now."

"Why?"

"Because of who—what—he is."

"You mean a wolf."

"No." Wade paused and looked at Jake. Silent communication passed between them. "He's a pack leader. Like his father was. It's a distinct line of our kind, and there are not many left."

I swallowed. "So you—you two—you're wolves, too."

They both laughed at that. "And you're not?" Wade said, smiling.

I shook my head. "Winter said—"

"That you're not a carrier. But you're still one of us, Tri. You just don't change. But there is much more to us than the change."

I could see them both looking at my arm, and I felt the bite-mark scars there pulse with heat.

"And you might change," Wade said, "now."

"All right," I said, "all right. But why hunt Ethan, even if he is a pack leader or whatever you said he was? How could he be a threat to something like—like." A horrible image flashed in my mind. I tried to push it back.

"It's a long story," Wade said, "that goes back hundreds of years. We don't have time for it now. But it comes down to free will. Our kind has a choice. To live this way or live like the weren. And the weren, of course, think theirs is the better way. Superior. They want ours to be a dying race."

"Oh." This was not a new idea. History—real history—was full of this. Religious wars. Genocide. What Hitler tried to do to the Jewish people. What we did to the American Indians. Darfur. "How many—of us—are left?" I asked.

Again Wade and Jake exchanged a look. "Enough," Wade said. "Enough for now. Someday we'll fade out, weren or no weren. They just want it sooner rather than later."

I thought about what Winter had said, how I had given her and my father hope, because I was not a carrier, and I wondered if this was the reason they had opted not to have children of their own. It seemed they didn't want this race to carry on.

Wade handed me some jerky, a tin cup of sweet, hot tea and a canteen of water. "You need to eat," he said.

"Thank you."

"We can't go back today," he said.

I nodded my head and beat back the hot sting of tears in my eyes. Then I realized something: Tabby.

"My aunt's a pilot," I said. "She'll search for me."

"Maybe," Wade said. "But she might figure out that you ran, and that if you're alive, you'll need to stay hidden."

"So when the moon's not so full we can go back?"

"No. They don't need the moon to be full to turn—the moon just has to be up, day or night. But they're most powerful when the moon is full or almost. That's why they're here right now. Generally they don't like to turn in the day—they don't like to be seen—but out here they're not gonna care."

"So the moon is set, now. We can go back when the moon is set, when they'll be normal."

"They're never normal," Jake said.

I looked at Wade. "Moon or no moon they're dangerous," he said. "But we really can't risk getting caught by the moon—not for a few days anyway."

I wondered what had happened, in that short time between when we saw the Hanns on the trail and when I'd arrived home. If only I'd been there—

"We didn't think they'd attack while it was still light," Wade said, as if he knew what I thought. "They might have smelled you—us—on the trail and hurried back to make their move while we were gone. Or in their absence they were found out and knew it."

"You were watching my house?"

"We were watching your house."

"For how long?"

"Long enough."

Where were they, I wondered, as I stared out my window at night? Lurking in the trees, back in the guest house shadows. How close did they dare come?

"How did you know—how did they know—Ethan was there?"

"He puts out a strong signal. It wouldn't be long before he was found."

"Why didn't Winter think that?"

"She did—it wasn't easy to stay off her radar. She was vigilant. But she missed, with the Hanns."

I looked down at the fire. "It was because we needed the money," I said. "Off season guests are few and far between." The money, I thought: the money. It must have clouded Winter's judgment. "So what do we do?" I asked.

"Right now we have a nice trail leading right to us," Wade said. "We have to crisscross our tracks, hope for snow and find somewhere to hide."

"We can't do this forever," I noted.

"They'll be weak at the new moon," Jake said, rising. "And we won't be." He turned off the camp stove; the blue flame protested then died. We broke camp and headed out.

For the rest of the day we moved, farther out then back in and out again, leaving our scent in some places and not in others, not knowing if we were being hunted, followed, stalked—not knowing.

Weak at the new moon, strong at the full. I tried to remember how it all went; I realized I never really thought much about the moon. But I knew the basics: it had phases, and the new moon phase was weeks away. And the waning of this full moon would be long and slow.

When we stopped for the day, we watched the moon rise from another high vantage point as it started to get dark.

"Old Gibbous," Jake said, referring to the moon's current phase. "Just starting to wane, but still nearly full."

It was cold and clear, the temperature steadily dropping. We had pitched camp in a patch of large spruce on an otherwise barren knoll. A fire would be too easily seen at night; the brothers had the small propane camp stove set up behind a thick tree where they melted snow and boiled water for hot tea and soup. The cold was pervasive, but I was strangely warmer than I should have been, and I noticed the scar where Ethan had bit me pulsed with heat. Still, it would be a long night.

"Go on to bed," Wade said to me. "You'll be warmer."

I knew he was right, and reluctantly I crawled into the tiny tent and slipped fully clothed into one of the sleeping bags. I didn't know how I would get through the night, but I fell asleep quickly though my rest was fitful. Sometimes I was aware that Wade was in the tent; sometimes Jake was there. Sometime near morning I awoke more fully and realized neither brother was in the tent with me. And I heard wolves howling.

I pulled myself out of the sleeping bag, grabbed my shotgun and crawled outside. It was still dark, but there was a faint lightening on the horizon. Wade and Jake were where I imagined they'd sat most of the night—on the edge of the trees, the view spread out below. I quietly came up beside them.

"Where are they?" I whispered. But even as I spoke I heard them, the lonely howls rising up from beneath the knoll.

The brothers looked at my gun. "You won't need to kill them," Wade said. "They're our brethren."

The gun was cold and heavy in my hand. I thought about the wolves in the woods. I thought about Su. "Su," I said aloud.

"She's not out there, Tri. These are different wolves."

"Do they know we're here?"

"Of course. They're telling us something. Something's coming."

"Something?" I pictured Dr. Hanns, the sharp teeth and wild eyes—

"It's not the weren," Wade said.

"Should we leave?" I asked.

"No," he said. "We'll wait and see."

Maybe it was Winter, I thought. Maybe she had lived and was looking for me.

Slowly the light spread, gray and blue like it is in the winter mornings. Jake and Wade exchanged a few inaudible words.

"What?" I asked.

"We hear something," Wade said. I listened. At first I heard nothing, but as I concentrated, I began to pick out a faint sound—a light hiss, a sound I recognized.

"It's a dog team!" I said in a fierce whisper. I felt a chill of fear on the back of my neck.

Wade nodded. "But it's not them," he said again.

We waited. Then down below we saw forms moving in the dim light: wolves running alongside the trail we had made. And then there was the dog team. And the dogs were all white.

"It *is* them!" I said.

"No—it's not them," Wade repeated. "It's their dogs all right, but not them."

"But if their dogs—"

"It's better we find out, than just running. The wolves want us to wait."

I could hardly breathe. All I wanted to do was start running or climb a tree—do something. If their dogs had found us, could Dr. Hanns and his wife be far behind?

"There's something in the sled," Wade said, looking through his binoculars. Another long moment passed. "It's Ethan!"

"Is he alive?" Jake asked, and Wade handed him their binoculars.

My heart pounded, and my knees shook. As badly as I wanted to know, I didn't want to know. Though I thought of the scene I had left behind at the house in every waking moment, it was taking on a dream-like effect, and now the reality of it was back in full force.

The brothers stood when the sled disappeared in a bend on the trail as it started the climb to where we were. I pulled myself up, leaning slightly on my gun to steady myself. Then the white faces of the mute dogs appeared over the lip of the knoll and came to a stop several yards away. My fear suddenly vanishing, I dropped my gun in the snow and ran toward the sled, falling down to my knees near the basket as my eyes took in the still white form of its silent passenger.

"Ethan," I said, touching his cold face. "Ethan."

Wade and Jake were on the other side of the sled basket. "He's alive," Jake said, touching Ethan's throat.

"He is?" I looked at the brothers and felt a rush of hope.

"Yes," Wade affirmed. "But he's not well."

"Is this a trick?" I asked, glancing in the direction the team had come.

"The dogs brought him to us," Wade said. "In their genetic memory they know we are connected, though their immediate instincts are that we're enemies, as dogs and wolves have become. But he must have communicated to them, and they obeyed."

"But these are Dr. Hann's dogs. Won't they find us now?"

"Yes—but more because of Ethan than the dogs. But we have to help him. He's dying."

The words were like cold hands on my throat, and I felt hope turning to fear and dread. Carefully the brothers lifted him from the sled. I followed wordlessly as they carried him to the tent. "We have to take off his clothes," Wade said as they laid him down on the sleeping bags. I backed away from the tent's entrance and waited. After a few moments Jake came back out.

"We have to warm him first," Jake explained. "Wade will stay with him. Let's tend to the dogs."

"Okay," I said weakly. At Jake's instruction I filled a pot with snow and put it on the lit camp stove. As the snow melted down I heaped more into it until the pot was full of water. In the meantime Jake unclipped the dogs one at a time from the line and found enough rope to tie each individually to a tree. "We'll give them water," he said, "then we'll cook them a pot of rice." I realized his mission was more than the dogs: he was keeping me occupied, and he was standing guard with a rifle strapped across his back. His actions took him in a constant circle around our small camp, which was no accident. The dogs were no comfort to me; I could see their fear. But were they afraid of us, or afraid of what might be following along the trail? I carried the pan of water from dog to dog, wondering how they and Ethan escaped from the Hanns. I petted each and kissed each on the forehead and thought of dear, dear Keats as I last saw him, lying still in a pool of blood.

While I rejoiced that Ethan lived, I was filled with a sense of impending doom. They were coming for us, now more than ever. And the moon was still nearly full. I thought of my life, the quietness of it, the dull routine of predictable repetition. And I longed for it like never before.

After I watered the dogs, Jake took the pot, melted more snow then mixed rice into the water. I watched him stir and was taken at once with how young he was. Distant and aloof, he had seemed much older than Wade, with his angular features and shifting eyes, though logically I knew he couldn't be.

"So do you have parents?" I asked.

He glanced at me quickly, then looked back to the rice. "Yes," he said. "A mother."

"Where is she?"

"Farther north," he said, and left it at that.

Then Wade emerged from the tent, and Jake moved to take his place. They exchanged a few quiet words before Jake slid into the tent. Wade crouched across from me.

"How is he?" I asked.

He shook his head. "I don't know. He has a lot of wounds."

"They'll be coming, won't they? And what do we do?"

Wade looked out at the distance beneath the knoll. "They're without their dogs. They'll have to find another way to travel. And maybe they have their own wounds to deal with. But yes, they'll be coming."

"So what do we do?"

He seemed to smell the air. "The wolves are still here. So they're not close, yet. We might have a day."

"Shouldn't we get a head start then?"

He nodded his head toward the tent. "We can't move him. Not right now. He's not strong enough. He needs to be still, and warm."

"Where will we spend the night?"

"If we last the day, then we should stay here. Where we can listen, and hopefully know if they're coming. To travel at night—they could catch us in the woods. It would be all over."

"There must be someone somewhere who can help us," I said.

"What helps us is time, Tri. We need to get to the new moon."

The day was long passing. Wade and Jake took turns warming Ethan with their bodies. I did what I could to help: making tea, re-watering the dogs, moving around to stay warm. Despite the endless day, night came too quickly, and before it was even fully dark we watched in silence as the moon rose again. Then Wade and Jake stepped aside and had a quiet discussion away from my ears.

"Tri," Wade said when they were finished. "Jake and I will keep watch. We need you to go into the tent and crawl in with Ethan." Even in the dark I could see the awkwardness on his face. He sighed. "You'll need to take off your clothes."

The blood rushed to my face, a strange shot of warmth in the pervasive cold. "What?"

"Your body needs to warm his," Wade explained. "That can't happen with clothes on. Just think of it as saving a life, not. . .anything else."

"Is he still naked?"

Wade turned his face. "Yes." We stood in silence for a moment before Wade continued. "Please Tri," he said. "Jake and I both need to be out here. Just in case. But he needs to be kept warm." He stepped closer to me, and I found his eyes in the dark. "Take your gun in there with you. If something happens out here, you'll know. Try to shoot them in the mouth. Break their teeth. Shoot at their hands."

"Wade—"

"We'll be right here. That's just in case. But they'll be hard pressed to get through me. I'll tear them to shreds first." He held my gaze. I felt something, coming from him. A kindness. And something more. If he had to, would he die to save me?

I turned to the tent. My hands shook as I opened the flap; inside it was dark and still, and Ethan lay on his back, encased in the sleeping bag. Even in the shadowy light I could see how he looked like death. I put down the shotgun, took off my boots and coat and slipped in beside him. I removed the rest of my clothes under the covers and shoved them to the bottom of the bag. I reached out and pulled my coat up over the top of us. Then I inched over and let my skin touch Ethan's.

He was so cold. I felt the heat from my body being sucked into his.

And I could feel his wounds, gashes in his skin. I felt myself trembling all over. I concentrated on Wade's words, about saving a life, how that's all this was. I turned on my side, facing him. Very carefully I draped my limbs over him, pressed my face up against his shoulder, and breathed deep the smell of him. "Please live," I whispered. "Please live."

Fourteen

Incredibly, there was a morning. I had been aware, as the night passed, of the sound of a rising wind. I heard it move through the tops of the tall spruce that circled our camp; I felt it puff against the nylon walls of the tent. I was also aware of a rising of the temperature in the half-awake, half-asleep state in which I spent most of the night, nearly naked beside a naked boy. I knew a cloud cover was rolling in, one which most likely would bring snow. Snow would help cover our trail, help us hide. For the second time I felt hope.

And this hope was realized as I crawled out of the tent and saw the first flakes beginning to fall in the gray-dark of the morning. I could make out the shadowy figures of Wade and Jake, sitting close together, and joined them at the edge of the camp.

"How is he?" Wade asked.

"I don't think he's much different," I said. "Is it because he lost so much blood?"

"Weren bites are bad, real bad. He's lost right now. He needs to recover enough to turn—and soon. Or he might become one of them."

For a moment I could only look at Wade. "You mean one of *them* them?"

"He needs to turn," Wade said again.

I remembered the wolf tracks in the blood trail from the kitchen. Winter. I figured she had turned to save herself—but from more than what I had imagined.

"How can we help him?"

"Only with what we're doing. But snow's coming. Lots of it. We need to move today. And we need to move him. They'll sense where he is, if they haven't already." Wade handled a small flashlight; I realized they were looking at a map.

"Where are we?" I asked, looking at the area they were

concentrating on.

"Here," Jake said, pointing. "More or less."

We were in the foothills of the Susitna Mountains: small in stature compared to the massive nearby Alaska Range, but formidable just the same. Climbing farther into them was not a good idea; returning the way we came, I assumed, was worse. But as I looked at the map, I had a thought. My family had an old cabin, in a valley to the southeast of where we were. We used to go there, when my dad was alive, but only Tabby had visited the place in recent years. The valley was tucked in and hidden and would not be seen from a distance. We could build a fire and get warm, maybe get Ethan's blood flowing again.

"My family has a cabin—here," I said, pointing to the spot on the map. "There would be wood for a fire."

Wade and Jake put their heads close. "It's pretty far," Wade said. "But it is go that way or head west. We could go that way. Maybe we'll find your cabin."

The brothers looked toward the tent. "Let's water the dogs," Wade said, "and get out of here."

We were busy for the next half hour, and the light—the blessed light—became stronger. We took care of the dogs, then Jake and I hooked up the team while Wade prepared Ethan for the journey. They decided to collapse the tent but keep Ethan inside it, bundled in the sleeping bags. Wade would run the team while Jake and I would ride on the snowmachine.

Again, I petted and soothed the frightened dogs. A few actually wagged their tails for me, but most just looked at me with sad, questioning eyes. "It's all right," I said over and over. "We're not going to hurt you."

"They like you," Jake said, hooking a dog up to the running line.

"Well, they don't look very happy."

"They can sense that you mean them no harm," he said. "They've known little kindness. And they can sense yours, even though they don't like our kind."

I still didn't feel I was included in that "our kind," but I let the matter slide. If I ever got to the point again where I saw my life stretched out before me, I would worry about it then. For now, a future—which I had once just assumed was mine—seemed like a golden ticket at the end of a long dark road.

I led the last dog over from the trees to the sled. She was small and white—delicate, a perfect creature of snow. Her blue eyes looked up into mine as I handed her over to Jake. He clipped her into her place on the lead-line, and I said a silent prayer for all of us.

"When does the moon rise?" I asked.

"The moon will rise just after five," Jake said. "But it hasn't set yet."

"What?"

"It will set just before two today," he said. "Then rise again just after five."

"Is it safe to travel?"

"No," he said flatly. "But we're not safe here. We'll stay in the open until two, even if we have to stop for a while, then we'll try to be where we're going by five. That's all we can do."

I nodded, but didn't have anything to contribute. I had no idea how long it would take us to reach the cabin. I had no idea if we could actually find it, even, but I felt in my heart that if we found the valley I would recognize it, though it had been many years since I had been there.

Wade called for Jake, and they carried the limp tent over to the sled and set it gently in the basket. It looked like we were transporting a body, and that thought made my skin crawl. "Can he breathe in that?" I asked.

The brothers looked at me and almost smiled, then nodded and finished loading both sleds. Then it was time to go. With my father's shotgun strapped across my chest, I climbed onto the cold snowmachine seat behind Jake. I looked back at Wade for a moment, ready on the runners of the dog team. He caught my eye and smiled slightly, and then we were off.

We traveled downward first, back the way we had come up the ridge, then we broke off our previous trail and cut through a valley which ran beneath the ridge where we'd camped. At times clusters of trees seemed dangerously close, then we broke out into a wide-open area—high country hills, barren save the occasional spruce. Caribou country. Wolf country. But today an empty land.

I looked over my shoulder and saw that Wade was falling behind. He seemed to be having trouble with the dogs. I tapped Jake's shoulder with a mittened hand, and he slowed to a stop. He let the snowmachine idle and we waited. But Wade was stalled. I got off the machine and began walking down the trail toward him.

"What is it?" I asked when I was within hearing distance.

"I don't know," he said. "But it's not good."

We looked in every direction. There was nothing. But the dogs looked as if they had a spell cast over them—they stood in their tracks unmoving, not looking at anything. I walked up to the lead dog and crouched down to her level.

"What is it, girl? Won't you come? Come on, come on, let's keep moving now." I petted her head and grabbed her collar, gently pulling her forward. Reluctantly the team followed, but the pace was slow. "Come on, come on!" I encouraged, trying to pick up my own speed. Wade stepped off the runners and came up beside me.

"There are wolves coming," he said.

"Regular wolves?"

He smiled. "Yes, regular wolves. But many. Can you keep pulling the dogs?"

I nodded, but my heart started beating fiercely. I looked behind me, down the miles we had come, and could now distinguish movement low on the horizon. Wade ran forward and talked to Jake, then ran back to his place at the back of the sled, where he jogged between the runners.

It didn't take long for the wolves to gain on us. I tried not to look behind me but soon a large dark form was beside me, a good equal for the black wolf that had been in my yard at home which seemed now like a lifetime ago. The wolf matched my pace and stayed there, and I held on to the poor lead dog and kept putting one foot in front of the other, hoping the dogs would continue to do the same. "It's all right," I began to whisper, over and over. "It's all right." The dogs increased their pace, and I was now moving at a steady jog, my breath coming out in white puffs. I kept thinking I would run out—of breath, of energy—but I didn't, and felt like I could run forever. Other wolves came into my line of vision—gray ones, multicolored ones, wolves with lots of white and silver-gray. I saw Jake look over his shoulder at Wade. I wondered what they thought. The stock of my father's gun bumped on my back as I ran, and though I knew I couldn't use it because maybe one of these wolves might be Su, I felt better for it being there.

I ran with the dogs. The wolves ran with me. The snow had thickened slightly, but the deep gray of the incoming clouds indicated what was to come. The snow could help us, but it could also trap us. The snow we *had* been traveling on was settled, packed, wind-blown, and hard; the snowmachine—especially if two of us were on it—could easily get bogged down in a few feet of fresh snow, and the dog team would need the snowmachine to break trail. But that was a problem for later. The problem now was that there was still a moon up there somewhere, hidden behind those ominous clouds, and the time for it to set would not come fast enough.

I don't know how I kept running. Miles must have passed; somehow my legs continued to move, and as the falling snow thickened the wolves around us were grainy ghosts gliding through a field of white. The high country rolled on. I felt the world was with us: the wolves, the snow, the terrain. Helping us. From what was out there somewhere, trying to find us.

Finally, my energy started to fade. My thighs felt like burning lead and my breathing was now in short, ragged bursts. Suddenly Wade, who had been running behind the team, was between me and the great black wolf that seemed my personal sentry.

"Ride the runners," he said. He reached in front of me, grabbed the lead dog's collar, and took my place. I could sense the lead dog's discomfort with Wade's close presence, but she kept running, and I gratefully hopped onto the runners at the back of the sled.

I had ridden on dog teams a number of times in my life and have always loved the feel of them, like gliding on snow. Though now the sound of Jake's snowmachine growled steadily in my ears, in other times I had been struck by the beautiful quiet a dog team provides— the sound of the runners hissing along the trail, the muffled pats of the paws the only sounds as you race through the woods.

Now that I was suddenly not moving, I was beginning to feel the cold. I alternately kept one foot on the runner and used the other to kick along the trail, helping to keep the sled moving along as well as getting my blood moving again. Again I noticed the strange warmth coming from the scar on my arm and was grateful for it.

The tent top under which Ethan lay was now shrouded in white. I prayed he still lived.

After we traveled for what seemed a long time, suddenly the great black wolf stopped running. My eyes held his as the sled hissed passed, and I watched over my shoulder as the other wolves gathered around him and the pack took off to the west. I felt a sense of loss, as well as a chill of fear. Did the wolves leave because the Hanns were on their way?

A short time later Jake stopped the snowmachine and the dogs slowed to a stop. I hopped off the runners and began checking the dogs, straightening harnesses and looking for bleeding cracks on their paws. Wade was breathless and paced around for a few minutes, and Jake quickly set up the camp stove and put on a pot of snow to melt before he and Wade approached me.

"The moon's down," Wade said. "But they're coming. They've been traveling as weren; out here they don't have to worry about someone seeing them."

"How do you know?" I asked.

"We just do," Jake said. "We can feel our enemies—sometimes."

"Are they close?" I asked, panic in my voice.

"Not yet," Wade said. "And now they've turned so they're essentially humans on foot. We have about three and a half hours before the moon comes up again, so we have to rest the dogs long enough to water them then get moving again."

"Why were the wolves following us?"

"To dilute Ethan's presence," Wade said. "But there was something else, too, some feeling I was getting from the alpha."

"Love," Jake said, the word sounding funny coming from him.

Wade nodded. "It was something like that. But they're on our side—that was for sure."

"Su?" I asked. "Do you think Su was there?" My heart twisted and leapt at once.

They both looked behind us to where the wolves vanished and shook their heads.

"But how do you know?"

"I think she would have stood out—I think we would have felt her," Wade said, and my heart sank back to where it seemed to live in this strange new world of mine.

While Jake watered the dogs, Wade reached his hand inside Ethan's many coverings. I waited, barely breathing.

"He's okay," Wade said. "Maybe he's a bit stronger than he was." He offered me an encouraging smile. For what seemed like the millionth time, I held back tears. Wade handed me the water canteen. "We'll find your cabin," he said. "Hopefully the snow and the wolves will cause enough confusion so we can rest a bit. Four more days, and they'll start to weaken. We need to make a plan, and be ready."

I nodded and drank from the canteen as Wade carefully adjusted

Ethan's coverings. Not for the first time I wondered what would have happened if Wade and Jake hadn't come into my life. I imagined that I would be dead now. Another day in history. I thought how Mr. Palmer would miss me if I died. Mr. Palmer, and Ms. Curtis. Emma. Jack. For the first time in forever I felt like my world was full of love— full of people who loved me, people to whom I mattered. And not least of which was Wade James, who handed me a granola bar and a few pieces of jerky and told me it was time to go.

I was back on the snowmachine now, blinking against the thickening snow. Our visibility was failing, but at one point we could see several caribou on a not-too-distant hill, punching through the snow with their long legs as they ran away from us. The country went on for miles, and I felt a twist of loneliness for us, way out here. It would be so easy to get lost, to not find your way back out if you were unprepared. People disappear in Alaska; it is as if the land swallows them up. But Jake had a compass taped to the front of the machine, and several times we stopped so we could consult the map.

Soon we began climbing upwards at a gradual angle. As we got higher I began to worry about avalanches, which could be triggered by snowmachines. But we had to go up before we could slip down into the valley where the cabin was, and it was a chance we had to take.

And just as the day was beginning to fade, we crested a high hill and looked down upon what appeared to be the valley we were seeking. But I couldn't see the cabin.

"The light's bad," Wade said. "And there's lots of snow. It could be there. If it's not, we'll cross to the other side. There's a gulley over there and we'll try to find a strategic place to camp."

It was a quick drop into the valley. Now we were racing against the fading light; the cabin would be impossible to find in the dark. But soon I saw a dark mass in the snow, and I tapped Jake's shoulder and pointed. It was the cabin—snow swept and almost buried—but there. We pulled up to the front, where an old wooden door flanked by twin windows formed an encouraging face of welcome. Wade and Jake grabbed shovels from the snowmachine sled and rapidly freed the doorway from the snow that had pressed up against it. Then they stood aside and let me be the first to enter. I slid the wooden latch and pushed the door inwards.

The place was dark and cold but had suffered no break-ins from assorted high-country animals. So it was clean, neat, with a corner stacked high with firewood, and cupboards where I knew we would find some dried food. There was a cubby with a bed in it, a set of bunk beds and a homemade corduroy couch. I felt a rush of memories; I could picture my dad coming in through the doorway, arms piled high with wood, laughing.

Wade and Jake wasted no time. Wade built a fire while Jake climbed onto the roof to remove the snowcap from the chimney. Then they carried Ethan inside and laid him on the couch, slipping him from the tent. Ethan remained pale, unmoving, and cool. I adjusted his covers and placed my hand on his cheek. As I did, I felt the scar on my arm pulse, and what felt like a current of energy seemed to run through me. I pulled back, startled. Wade and Jake both looked at me—as if they had felt it, too—then they quickly turned away.

I sat by Ethan as the cabin warmed and as Wade and Jake tended to the dogs. I tentatively touched his still face again and kept my hand there even as I felt a strange sensation move through my arm, tracing my fingers lightly over his features. There was an instant where it seemed he felt me; there was no movement, but his face shifted somehow, for an instant. But perhaps it was only a trick of the dim light. Perhaps it was only my hopeful heart.

Wade came in and began building a fire in the wood cook stove. "I can do that," I said quietly.

"I've got it," Wade said. "Stay."

His eyes met mine from across the room. A strange moment passed. Then I asked, "Does your mother know—about you and Jake?"

"Yes."

"Is she like you?"

"Yes. Only she—has difficulty controlling it. It's best she doesn't live near too many people."

"Is she a weren?"

"No!" he said. Then he looked back to the cook stove. "We would have killed her if she were."

Then Jake walked in and said, "Moon's up." I tried not to think about what that meant.

I was soon to find out.

Fifteen

A short while later, while the cabin bathed in the soft yellow glow of the kerosene lamps, Ethan began to moan. The cool hand I held in mine began to shake. Wade and Jake left the table and came to my side.

"What's wrong?" I asked.

"He wants to turn," Wade said. He looked at Jake. "He feels the moon."

Jake shook his head. "That's not good. That's not good."

"You don't mean—he's not—"

"Not yet," Wade said. "But he's got to turn. Turn the right way, I mean."

"Can we do anything?" I asked.

"No," Wade said. "We're doing all we can."

Soon Ethan quieted, and his hand now gripped mine fiercely. Wade and Jake stood near the door, talking quietly.

"Should we board the windows?" I heard Wade ask Jake.

"Might be a good idea. If we can find some things to board them with." They looked at me.

"Outside under the cubby," I said. "There's usually old boards and stuff out there. Or in the woodshed. And there should be a tool chest, in a cupboard by the door." I wondered if boarding the windows would even help.

"It might buy a few seconds," Wade said. Could he read my thoughts, I wondered, and not for the first time.

So Wade and Jake boarded the windows, then they brought in all nine of the dogs. We would let the fire die, and after all other preparations were made, we blew out the lights. And then we waited.

Sometime, and somehow, I fell into a dreamless black sleep, my head on the couch near Ethan's quiet chest, then I heard something, and an image of Ethan flashed across my consciousness as I woke to a strange, animalistic sound. The couch was empty.

My heart leapt. I sat up and searched the dark of the cabin. Then Jake appeared near me. "It's Ethan," he whispered. "He's turning."

As my eyes adjusted to the dark, I could make out figures by the door, one standing—Wade—and the other in a ball on the floor, struggling. Scattered about the room were the ghostly white shapes of the dogs; I could feel their paralyzing fear.

"Ethan!" I whispered, then Jake's hand covered my mouth.

"Don't call him back," he said. "He needs to go."

I heard the sliding of the wooden latch, then a gust of cold blew into the room as Wade opened the door and Ethan slipped outside into the wind and the snow.

Jake took his hand away from my mouth. "He'll freeze!" I said.

"He's turning," Jake said.

"Turning into what?"

"We don't know yet."

"How will we know?"

"Well, if he becomes a weren, he should return shortly and kill us."

I began to shake. I didn't know whether to scream or cry. He would stay Ethan, I told myself. He would not let himself become a monster.

Wade came over and we three sat together on the couch, all with our guns, listening. And so the hours passed.

Again I don't know how I did it, but somehow I dozed off. When I opened my eyes again it was light, and Wade sat at the table while Jake slept on the bunk. Through the gaps in the boards that crisscrossed over the windows I could see that it still snowed outside—thickly, fiercely.

A fire burned in the stove; I could feel the wonderful warmth. Only three of the nine dogs remained inside. I stood and walked quietly over to Wade.

"What's going on?" I whispered.

"If the Hanns are out there, they'll be chasing Ethan now. There's been enough snow to completely cover our trail, so we're betting we can hold tight here—at least until the moon sets. Then we'll need to decide if we go again or not."

"Ethan didn't come back," I said.

"That's a good sign," Wade said. "We can hope."

I thought about how densely the snow was falling, and how Ethan was out there in it—the wind and the snow. "What about when he turns back? Won't he freeze?"

"Hopefully he'll find his way back here when he feels himself starting to turn."

"What do you do, when you turn?"

"What do I do? Try to remember who I am, try not to let it take total control of me. Try to remember where I left my clothes."

"Did you and Jake kill Dan's dogs?"

"Dan?" It took him a moment to remember. "Oh—your neighbor. The trap-man."

"Wolves killed two of his dogs. Was that you?" Or Ethan, I wondered but did not say.

"No, Tri, I'm afraid that was Su."

"Su?" A flush of alarm rushed through me. "No—it couldn't be." And I realized I really didn't know. I remembered Winter's hesitation, when I asked her if Su had turned yet.

"It's all right, Tri. I am sorry about the dogs, but Su didn't mean it. The first couple of times you turn, there's not a lot of control. I'm sure once she understands, nothing like that will happen again. We're not killers, Tri." He handed me a cup of hot black tea, poured from a kettle on the table. "Here," he said. "It's good."

My hands shook as I drank.

"To Su, it would have been like a dream. She wouldn't have remembered. Tri—" His hand touched mine. I felt the warm press of it. "It will be okay."

There was something besides friendship and concern in his touch. I looked at our hands, there, joined. For a moment I felt a longing to keep mine in his. Then I remembered Ethan's desperate grip in the night, the way I stared at his beautiful wounded face, hour after dark hour. I slowly slipped my hand from Wade's and looked away from his earnest gaze.

"Can you read my thoughts?" I asked quietly.

"Not exactly. I can sense your emotions, sense what you're thinking."

What look must have crossed my face then, I could only imagine.

"You are safe with me, Tri," he whispered. "Inside and out."

Jake stirred and sat up on the bunk. "It's almost noon," he said. Wade was slow to respond. I said, "When does the moon set?"

"A little after two," Wade said. "Then it comes up at seven."

"When is the new moon?"

"The twenty-seventh. Thanksgiving."

"Thanksgiving?"

"Hopefully we'll have something to be thankful for."

The plan, for now, was to hold tight in the cabin. Time ticked slowly by as we waited out the day, with the relief on the brothers' faces visible when the hour moved past two. We talked of the Hanns as Wade and Jake cleaned and checked their rifles.

"Did you know of them before now?" I asked.

"Yes," Wade said. "I mean, we've known about a male and a female in the Merlin River area."

"How?"

"Disappearances."

"Disappearances?"

"People disappearing, bodies not turning up."

"I thought that was because of murderers—serial killers."

"The Hanns *are* serial killers. All weren are. But they eat their victims—every last bit but the bones—so there are no bodies, just missing people."

"They do this every month?"

"No, no—once in a blue moon, you might say. And when they feel threatened. And when people make them angry."

I thought of Winter and Su. Did they escape that awful fate?

"Su had turned, and then she ran," Wade said quietly. "And Winter likely turned. As wolves we're pretty good at evading them"

"Then if you and Jake turned, you'd be safer."

He didn't answer. I looked at him. "You and Jake could turn, go out there and find Ethan, and be safer than you are now, here with me. Right?"

He held my gaze. "We're not leaving you, Tri."

"But you could—should."

"Look," he said. "There's no running—for any of us. Their target, their priority is Ethan, sure—but they know we know who they are. Even if they caught Ethan, they'd have to find us, too. We're loose ends. The weren don't like loose ends. And they're right not to like loose ends like us. Jake and I intend to kill them. No one is safe with weren in the world."

I remembered his words, how he would have killed his mother if she were a weren. "Have you done this before?"

"Yes."

"So you're—killers, weren killers."

"You could put it like that," Jake said. "But it's not like we *like* it or anything."

They went back to cleaning their rifles, sorting bullets, sharpening knives. I looked between the cracks of the boarded-up windows at the still-falling snow and counted the hours left until moonrise.

☽

Wade was kissing me. Or was he? I found myself wondering if I was awake or asleep, if this feeling of closeness, of sudden desire, was real. His shoulders were strong and broad, his hands—so gentle. He was warm and he smelled so warm, so warm and familiar. All around us the snow swirled down.

I opened my eyes. I was alone on the couch, a blanket twisted around me. The room was dark. But I could see Wade, sitting on the bunk, watching me. He put his fingers to his lips, motioning me to be quiet. He held his gun. Jake was pressed against a wall near the door. I heard the sad sounds of the voiceless dogs. They were scared. My heart all but stopped. Something was out there.

Sixteen

I could see movement through the boards covering the window— darker shadows on the shadows. Wade and Jake were still with rifles raised, their eyes moving from window to door to window to door. My own shotgun was out of reach, and I longed for it as I sat frozen, waiting.

Then a voice broke the silence: "It's Winter!"

Wade and Jake looked at me. "It's her," I said, my heart leaping.

"Ask her something," Jake said.

"Who named Keats?" I said toward the door.

"You did, Tri."

"Why?"

"Because his birthday was the same as the poet John Keats. Halloween. And because you were sad John Keats died so young."

I looked at the brothers. "It's her," I said again.

Jake slid toward the door and cautiously pulled the latch. And out of the darkness stepped Winter.

"Tri," she said and embraced me. "Oh, Tri!"

As Wade and Jake relit the lamps I saw how ragged she was, with great wounds on the side of her face that had not yet healed.

"Where's Su?" I asked.

"I don't know." Wade pulled out a chair for her and as she sat Jake handed her a mug of water. "But I'm looking for her."

"She's alive?"

"She's with the wolves that were around our house."

"How do you know?"

"I've been tracking them."

"Here? Are they around here?"

She shook her head. "No. I lost the trail in the snow. But I'll find them again."

"What happened to Keats?"

"Dan found him. The Hanns had cleaned up—erased, for the most part, what had happened. But Dan found Keats in the woods not far from the house. He'll be all right, in time."

The words filled my heart. Wade sat down beside Winter. "How close are the weren?" he asked.

"Twelve miles to the east."

Wade and Jake exchanged a look.

"But they're moving north."

"We should leave," Jake said.

"I'll take the dogs with me," Winter said. She looked at Wade and Jake. "Trileka will be safer with you." Something passed between the three of them. Wade and Jake nodded. Then Winter said, "You're the hunters from up north." They nodded again. "So young," she said. "I should have guessed, but I didn't. Can you get Tri back to town?"

Jake said, "We're going after the weren."

"You'd be foolish not to wait," Winter said. "But you must know that."

"We know that," Wade said. "We can take Tri."

How could I just go back, I wondered, when nearly everyone I loved was out here?

"There's a lake," Winter said. "About a day's travel to the south. And there's a fishing cabin my husband had used for his flying business. There's a radio phone in there. Call Tri's aunt Tabby and have her come get her."

Jake pulled out his map and spread it over the table. All the miles and miles. Where in all that was Su—where was Ethan?

Winter traced her finger over the lines, showing the brothers the way. "I'll keep looking for Su," Winter said. "And you'll be able to find the weren soon enough."

"But what about Ethan?" I asked. "He's out there, too."

Winter looked at me. "Ethan has to survive or not, Tri."

"Isn't there anything we can do?"

My question received no reply, and soon we were getting ready to depart.

☽

The first hint of light was peeking over the horizon when we gathered outside the cabin ready to go. Winter had collected a small stash of supplies from the cabin and stood with a pack on her back and snowshoes strapped to her mukluks. She would have to break trail for the dogs, which she would lead with a rope attached to the front of the team.

Our plan was for both Wade and Jake to go in front on snowshoes, breaking trail, and for me to follow with the snowmachine. Wade wasn't comfortable with me bringing up the rear, but with both of them packing down a trail there would be less risk of getting the snowmachine stuck in the foot or so of fresh snow. Fortunately, I was no stranger to snowmachines and didn't have to worry about my ability to drive one.

I said goodbye to Winter. "Think good thoughts," she said. She gripped me in a fierce embrace. "I didn't know. . .everything there was to know about Ethan. But I knew about his father." She withdrew from me, a strange look crossing her face. "I loved him once," she said, "but my sister did, too."

And so the silence between them, I thought.

"I'm so very sorry all this has happened," she said.

I couldn't tell her it was okay.

"Be careful, Tri, and stay on your toes."

"Please find Su," I said.

"I will, Tri. I promise you." She hugged me again and walked off into the morning, the dogs reluctantly following. Then Jake started the snowmachine.

"Time to go," he said.

I noticed Wade lean a small canvas bag against the door. "Ethan's clothes," he said. "He'll come back for them, when he needs them."

I wanted to touch the bag, but Wade—all ready to go with his snowshoes strapped on—handed me my gun and indicated it was time to move. "Remember, the jaw and the hands. Shoot for the jaw and the hands."

I nodded and strapped the gun across my chest. Wade turned and hurried after Jake, and the two moved at a steady clip in front of me. I kept the machine at a low throttle except for those moments when I felt it begin to sink into the snow, and we left the cabin behind.

We traveled first through a small canyon to get out of the valley, then we headed straight south, away from the high country, toward the massive stretch of thick forest below.

I didn't know how Wade and Jake kept moving. I kept expecting them to stop and rest, but that didn't happen until a number of hours had passed and we reached the beginning of the woods.

We entered the area enough to feel somewhat sheltered and hidden inside the trees, then Wade and Jake lifted up their hands for me to stop and then they both collapsed, breathless, sitting in the snow with their backs against the trunks of trees, their snowshoes sticking up in front of them.

I turned the machine off and took the water canteens over to them. They drank, and their breathing steadied. After a few minutes Wade said, "Listen."

I froze. But I heard nothing. It was quiet.

"Yeah," Wade said. "It's quiet. Very quiet."

"What does it mean?"

"The weren have been here, and not too long ago. Recent enough so that their evil energy still lingers in the woods, scaring everything else away."

"They're such poison," Jake said. "They could have been miles from here but still be too close for the animals."

"How long 'til moonset?" Wade asked his brother.

Jake looked at his watch. "Two hours. Two hours, twelve minutes."

Wade huffed. Jake's eyes narrowed. "Two choices: speed or stealth," he said.

Wade nodded. "Drop the machine. Hope Tri can keep up." He flashed me a smile.

"Keep the machine and go faster," Jake said.

"Wait out the rest of the moon or keep moving," Wade said.

"We'd better give it some thought," Jake said. Wade nodded. They both closed their eyes and seemed to almost doze. I looked around at the still, quiet winter woods.

Were they here?

Wade opened his eyes. "If we drop the snowmachine and keep moving, it would be about the same as if we waited out the moon then traveled with the machine. So the real question is, are we safer without the machine? Will they hear it?"

"We've got a good stretch of time, from moonset to moonrise," Jake said. "About seven hours."

"That helps," Wade said. He took off his mittens and rubbed his eyes. "I think what we should do is this: rest awhile then take the machine. If we left it, they might find it and then they could use it."

"Right," Jake said.

"We'll just have to take the chance that between now and moonset they don't pin-point our location. They'd want to circle. If we stuck to the edge of the woods, they couldn't circle without us seeing them."

"Right," Jake said again. "I'll rest first." He closed his eyes and seemed to instantly fall into a light sleep. Wade motioned for me to sit next to him.

"Back against the trunk," he whispered. "And keep your gun ready."

I knew what they'd meant about the weren wanting to circle. It was a wolf instinct, to circle, for a pack to circle a herd. They divide, disperse like points on a clock, circle, and close in.

We sat unmoving while Jake rested. Then Jake opened his eyes, and Wade shut his. Each minute was agonizingly long, the woods quieter than I had ever known. Nothing moved, nothing breathed, no birds sang or flew past, no squirrels chattered in distant trees. It was as if the forest had been stripped of life.

But soon we were off again, the brothers tramping down a trail between the trees and me doing my best to keep the snowmachine on track. I felt as if every tree could be hiding one or both of the Hanns, and my back felt prickly and alive as if something were literally breathing down its length. The woods—which I had loved my whole life—seemed sinister now, like in a grim fairy tale, and I wondered how I would ever feel at ease walking in the forest again. Through the passing trees I saw the more open space which we had left behind, my thoughts invaded by ideas of wolves and werewolves and circles and points on a clock.

Eventually, we had to turn deeper into the woods. I saw Jake check his watch and say something to Wade. I thought they might stop, but they kept going, and I noticed they increased their surveying of the woods on either side and in back of us. I did the same. Soon we were surrounded by trees. Then after a tense half hour, Wade and Jake stopped, high-fived each other and turned to me with smiles on their faces which could only mean one thing: moonset.

Now they rested, giving themselves a little more time and deciding to do it at once instead of taking turns. I was to stand guard. I sat on the snowmachine seat with my shotgun in hand, listening to the still-quiet woods, fearing the emergence of any sound.

When they woke up, Wade and Jake looked at the compass and

consulted their map, then we began again. I tried to enjoy the reprieve from imagining werewolves behind every tree, but the easing of those thoughts simply brought others. Where was Su? And had she run out of time, I wondered, and would she always, now, be a wolf?

And Ethan was there, too, in my thoughts, the memory of his wounded body next to mine still burning within me, the feel of him as we pressed against each other by the back door still vivid and alive. Would I ever see him again?

I looked at Wade, there, ahead of me, and I remembered the dream I had about him. If he could sense my thoughts, could he sense my dreams?

More hours passed, and the sky took on that shade of blue that harkens the sinking of the sun and the emergence of the coming night. Gradually the light faded and stars began to appear in the sky, sparkling like crystals through the tops of the branches of the frozen trees. When the moon rose, I knew, everything would sparkle, the frost on the trees and the snow on the ground catching the light. I used to love that, that magical part of winter, the cold sparkling nights. How could the moon, the beautiful friendly lantern of the night, be the source of strength for something so evil? Was it the light—reflected sunlight—that feeds the werewolves, or was it that other force, the force that dictates the tides and has, on occasion, been blamed for the bad behavior of people? A combination of both? *Don't go out tonight, it's bound to take your life—there's a bad moon on the rise.* My father used to sing that song—Credence Clearwater Revival. Though he was cheerful and reassuring when he sang, I knew now that those words held a whole different meaning for him.

Despite the darkness I could see how the woods were beginning to become familiar to me. Home was somewhere to the south, and the thought of being so close to it twisted my heart. But the steady pace the brothers kept was indicative of the fact that we were far from any sort of safety.

Then all at once we came out of the woods and burst out onto the openness of snow-covered ice. Ahead of us, on the far shore, waited the fishing cabin, and within minutes I was pulling the snowmachine up near its front door. In the tradition of many bush-Alaskan cabins, the door was unlocked, and we slid the wooden latch and went inside.

I found the radio phone at its spot on a corner of the rough wooden table. Wade turned on his headlamp so I could see; it took me a few minutes to remember how to work it, but soon I could hear a ringing on the other end of the line, a ringing in Tabby's house. I took a deep breath and waited.

"Hello?" Sydney's voice came through, crackling in the static.

"It's Tri!"

"Tri! My God! Are you all right?"

"Yes. I'm at the fishing cabin."

"Is Winter there, too?"

"No—she's looking for Su. I'm with the James brothers. They saved me."

"It's Tri!" I heard him say, then Tabby was quickly on the line.

"Tri, tell me what's going on."

"I'm with the James brothers. We're at the fishing cabin. Winter found us at the mountain cabin and she's out there somewhere looking for Su. The Hanns might be after us. We don't know. Winter wants you to come get me."

There was a pause. "I can't safely land, Tri, until the moon is up—really up. But I'll be there, so be ready."

"Yes, Tabby."

"Are you all right?"

"Yes."

"I'll be there as soon as I can."

We waited in cold and darkness, listening for sounds, watching the windows. There was a supply of gas in the woodshed, and we'd filled the snowmachine and the jugs on the sled. I wondered how far it would take the brothers after we parted.

"Where will you go?" I asked, in a near whisper. Wade stood close to me against a wall near a window as the light from the moon began to illuminate the cold blue-black night.

"Back the way we came," Wade said. "Get back to the high country, wait out the moon."

"And then what?"

"Look for Ethan. Look for *them*."

I felt I could hear his heart. I closed my eyes for a moment, aware of his quiet breathing beside me. "Be careful," I said.

"We will."

I took off my mitten and let my hand find his. "Thank you," I whispered. Across the room Jake scanned the lake with a pair of binoculars. Then I heard Wade's breathing stop. He tipped his head a little, listening.

"What is it?" I whispered.

"I don't know." He released my hand and slipped outside, only to quickly rush back in.

"They're coming," he said.

"How—"

"Sometimes I can feel them. I feel them now. They're coming. They're almost here."

Seventeen

Jake tossed me my shotgun and I caught it with one hand. Then we were rushing out the door.

I didn't ask what the plan was, I just followed. We hurried into the woodshed, which had a small upper loft. We climbed and up and pulled the ladder up behind us, carefully closing and locking the trap door. I had always wondered why the shed had this loft. Now I felt I might be finding out.

There was a slit just big enough for a rifle barrel cut into the log work at the end of the loft facing the cabin. We slid on our stomachs over to it and looked out. There was nothing at first, just the cabin in the moonlight. Then I caught a blur of movement, then another, and then I could see how two fast moving creatures were circling the house, trying to glimpse in through the windows, trying to find the quickest way in. . .

I trembled with fear but then quickly got a grip on it. I didn't want them to feel me, sense my fear. Wade and Jake were on either side of me. I tried to tune in to their emotions. I felt their strength, their steadiness, their controlled anger. I pulled it into me. I felt my pulse steady.

Then I heard the plane, distant at first but rushing ever closer. I knew Tabby would make a direct landing, as stealth as possible, not chancing a fly-over. And so it was. We heard the plane come down on the ice, saw glimpses of the lights on its wings. And the monsters heard and saw it, too. I saw them turn as if in slow motion, saw their legs start to move toward the lake.

"Go," Jake said. "Go, go, go!"

Someone grabbed me by the back of the coat and yanked me away from the view-slit. Wade ripped open the trap door and dropped down, forgetting the ladder. Jake shoved me down after Wade—who caught me—and dropped down behind me. We ran. We ran out of the woodshed and around to the front of the house where the snowmachine sat. Wade yanked the pull cord and the machine growled to life. I hopped on behind Wade—clutching my father's shotgun—and Jake hopped on, his back to me and his front facing the rear, and Wade twisted the throttle and the machine screamed forward.

I looked over to Tabby's plane, taxiing on skis toward the cabin, the monsters almost reaching it. Turn back, I prayed. But it was the monsters who turned, hearing the snowmachine, and now they rushed toward us. Tabby revved her plane, and it lunged forward, cutting in front of the monsters. We raced across the frozen ice. I could hear Tabby's plane, revving forward then falling back, again and again, and the dark woods grew close then swallowed us up. Again I prayed for Tabby, but it was several long minutes before I heard the sharp sound of her plane taking flight, and I glimpsed it briefly, overhead, as it swooped above us then turned back toward town.

Now it was just us, the snowmachine, the trees and the night and the monsters on our tail.

Trees flew past as we raced down the trail we had made earlier that day—a trail I now realized was saving our lives. As fast as the weren were, the snowmachine was faster. As he rode backwards behind me, Jake pulled a headlamp from his coat pocket, put it on, and let its light shine onto the trail. He held his rifle ready. I held tight to my shotgun and wondered if I would be able to get it in position quick enough to use it if I needed to. How many shots I'd be able to get off.

At one point I felt Jake lift his rifle, and I waited for the sharp crack of a discharge. But it didn't come, and he lowered his gun. False alarm. I hoped.

After a time I could see clear spaces in the moonlight beyond the trees and we broke out of the woods and into the open country that led up to the foothills. Wade twisted the throttle more and the machine soared forward at an incredible speed.

Dawn broke. We stopped briefly to refuel the machine. While Wade did this, Jake scanned the horizon with his binoculars. He took them from his eyes and looked at Wade. "We've got about fifteen minutes," he said. I felt my heart thump and looked; I saw nothing.

"Then we'd better get going," Wade said.

One thing the brothers didn't mention but was heavily on my mind: The trail we'd made ended at the mountain cabin, and there were hours to go before moonset.

Though they didn't say it, I could feel that they felt it. There was a somberness now enveloping us, and I caught Wade more than once looking at the lightening sky as if it were that last time he would see it. I tried to do the same. I thought about Su and hoped that she would be rescued from the wolves. Winter, Tabby, and Sydney would take good care of her, and I tried to imagine her at eighteen, going to the prom, graduating from River Valley, then later at twenty or so, a flight attendant like she wanted to be, in her flight attendant suit, taller now and slender, her hair piled high on her head, laughing with the other flight attendants as she boarded a plane heading someplace wonderful. I pictured that place: Paris. I pictured Su in Paris, crossing a watery street in the rain, finding shelter in a café filled with the smells of hot coffee and fresh bread. She would laugh at the rain that fell from her umbrella as she closed it and take a seat by the window. And she would see her reflection and smile.

All this that was happening now would be long ago and far away, a dream that wasn't the happiest. She would send giant-sized postcards to Winter and Tabby, who would both have streaks of gray in their hair.

How would she remember me? I realized I had no idea, no clear image of what I was to Su.

And so I steeled myself for what was to come.

Shortly before we reached the mountain cabin, Wade stopped the snowmachine in the middle of the canyon through which we'd passed as we'd left the valley. There was a flurry of activity as the brothers grabbed the extra rifles out of the gear on the sled and stuffed their pockets with bullets.

"Let's go!" Jake said, and we turned to one side of the canyon and slogged through the snow toward a near vertical wall. Wade led the way. As we began to climb the steep snowy slope, he reached back and grabbed my hand, pulling me along.

I felt like I was scrambling. Loose rocks and snow fell out from under my feet and tumbled down behind me. We kept climbing— crawling—up the slope. Then we came to a lip of a ledge that jutted out from the increasingly vertical face of what now seemed more cliff than slope.

"This looks good," Jake said from just below me. Wade and I pulled ourselves onto the flat, snowy surface and Jake quickly joined us.

I didn't want to look, but I did. In the gray morning light I could see them, two moving shapes, still aways away but closing the distance fast.

Jake handed me the binoculars. "Do you want to look?"

"I don't know."

"It's best to know your enemy," Jake said.

I looked. The creatures ran on all fours with a leaping sort of motion. They had big, humped backs, but I realized it was something they were wearing. "What's on their backs?" I asked.

"Their clothes," Jake said. "They have good control over when they turn, and they'll carry clothes with them, so they never have to back-track before turning into their human form."

I handed Jake the binoculars and fought back the terror that wanted to swallow me whole. Wade and Jake set us up on the ledge: Wade to the left, Jake to the right, me in the middle. Loaded guns and boxes of bullets were placed on either side. Then we stood and waited. "Wait to shoot," Jake said, "until they're close. I'll tell you when. We'll have a short time to get in some good hits and knock them back. But they'll recover fast. So we have to keep knocking them back."

I nodded, holding tightly onto my father's shotgun.

"Don't focus on them," Wade said. "Don't let yourself get consumed by their awfulness. Concentrate on stopping them. Believe in the power of your gun."

"Okay," I said. "I'll try."

My heart thundered in my chest as I watched the creatures get closer and closer and closer still. Beneath their vests muscled limbs covered with coarse looking mud colored fur pulsed with sinewy strength. Soon I could see their angry canine faces—snarling lips and teeth-filled jaws. Oh, God, I wanted my father. I wanted Tabby, I wanted Winter, I wanted Sydney, I wanted somebody to say, *Wake up!*

They tore past the snowmachine and looked up at us, perched on our ledge. They paused only a second before tackling the slope—more easily than we did—and I knew we were looking at a mere minute or two.

Jake raised his hand. "Hold," he said, "but take aim."

We lifted our guns and pointed them down the slope. I caught one in my sites—was it Mr. Hanns or Mrs. Hanns, I wondered. I pulled in some deep breaths. Jake kept his hand up.

"Hold. . .hold. . .ho—"

Then out of nowhere the cry of a lone wolf filled our ears. The

Hanns stopped and turned, their attention diverted. Down below a great wolf stood—white and silver-gray with bits of black.

It was a wolf I knew. "Ethan," I said.

The Hanns began leaping back down the slope.

"Shoot!" Jake said even as his own gun fired. And for a moment the sound of gunfire split the air. As I squeezed my trigger my eyes diverted to the wolf down below, and I caught his gaze for a fraction of a second as he turned and loped speedily away, the weren running after.

We stood in the smell of gunpowder with ringing ears. There were streaks of blood on the snow but the weren seemed unfazed as we watched the race below until the pursued and the pursuers were out of sight.

At that point I sat down, leaned my back against the rocky face, and tried to steady my shaking.

"What now?" I managed to ask.

"We wait," Wade said. "Wait for that dammed moon to set."

"Okay."

He sat beside me. "Are you all right?" he asked.

I nodded. I didn't want to talk about it. I closed my eyes. I felt Wade's arm go around my shoulders and I didn't try to stop it. After a while I fell into a deep sleep and dreamt of being in a small, closed space. I was crawling. It was warm and cold at once; I could smell dirt, and I could smell cool fresh air. It was dark. In front of me I could see Ethan, his pale face and his dark hair.

"Trileka Tyler," he whispered and touched his forehead to my forehead, his nose to my nose. I wanted his lips, felt mine slide to the side of his, almost there but not quite.

"Don't go to him," he said, and suddenly we were back in the entry at home, before the real nightmare began, and I wanted to shout for joy but then I was pulled from there, and when my eyes opened sluggishly I felt for a moment that I had woken up to a different dream—I couldn't remember where I was and everything seemed strange and hazy. A pot of water bubbled on the camp stove and a warm sleeping bag lay over my legs. My head rested on a big, strong shoulder. Then I remembered—slowly as if my brain were protecting me—the events of the night and the morning, along with mixed fragments of my recent dream.

Don't go to him.

I straightened and Wade pulled his arm out from behind me.

"Feel better?" he asked.

I nodded but found it hard to look at him. Could he know my dreams? Could Ethan? My head hurt and I realized I was very thirsty.

"Here." Jake squatted in front of me, handing me a cup of hot sweet black tea.

"Thank you," I said, and sipped it gratefully. It tasted better than anything I could remember.

Wade stood and stretched.

"Do we know anything?" I asked.

"No," Wade said. "It's been quiet."

"How long until the moon goes down?"

"An hour or so."

"What will we do then?"

"Jake and I thought we could stop at your cabin and recharge for a few hours, but before dark we'd better set up a camp someplace high where we can defend ourselves. There's no sense trying to hide, so we'll build a big fire and stay ready."

So after moonset we gathered our things and made our way down the steep knoll. I tried not to touch the bloody places in the snow or look at the weren's ghastly tracks. We rode the snowmachine the short distance to the cabin, and I noticed the bag of Ethan's clothes still leaning by the door.

"It was just yesterday, we left those there," Wade said. "He hasn't been turned too long yet."

We went inside, built a warm fire, and Jake slept while Wade and I cooked dried soup and made tea. I felt drained and exhausted, but my headache had receded, and I sat on the soft couch by the fire and soaked up as much comfort as I could. I knew it wouldn't last long.

"These are simple, good things," Wade said quietly. "Food. Warmth."

I repeated that in my mind: *Simple, good things.* Something I had never realized.

Eighteen

Light was fading by the time we left the cabin; the sun was setting just after four in the afternoon, and the hours of daylight were shrinking as we slid toward the winter solstice in December. Six months from now we'd experience the opposite, the days growing longer and longer until the light lasted all night on summer solstice. When Su and I were little, there was a big summer solstice barbeque in town that we'd go to with Winter and our dad. Everyone would be there, and there would be plenty of food, and local musicians would play their instruments. Su and I would join hands and dance sometimes, and if it was cold and rainy we'd wear our tall rubber boots and our raincoats, and the grown-ups would build a fire so people could get warm. But on the blue-sky solstices the sun would beat down on us, in the little village park, for hours and hours until it would finally slip below the horizon and the bugs would come out and the evening would cool. I could remember sitting on my dad's lap at the end of one such evening, smells from the barbeque still lingering in the air, and him brushing the mosquitoes off my sunburnt arms as I hovered near sleep. Then he carried me, and Winter carried Su, and they said goodnight to all our friends and loaded us up into the Subie—which was much newer then and shone in the last rays from the sun.

Now, the cold air from the fading day was blasting my face as I rode behind Jake on the snowmachine while Wade took a turn pounding down a trail with a pair of snowshoes. We had roughly six hours before moonrise; we were all feeling a little tired, so we moved slower than we had these last couple of days. We moved through and out of the canyon, then found a spot where we could climb at a diagonal up to the top. At this point I put on snowshoes and followed behind Jake. As the light faded the world turned a crystal blue. And it was getting colder by the minute.

We moved until we found a tight cluster of trees to help break the wind that would likely hit us up high like this. In front of us the canyon dropped sharply, and in back of us and beyond the group of trees the land was flat, white, and open for some time. The Hanns would not be able to sneak up on us, and I knew that was the point. Jake had loaded the sled with wood from the cabin's woodshed, and while Wade pitched the tent, I helped Jake make a fire. We stretched some extra tarps across some trees to make a wind-block, and within a short time we managed to create a feeling of shelter in the wide night as we laid some more tarps across the snow and put down some bedding so we could sit by the fire. Our backs were to the dangerous canyon edge, and we faced out toward the desert-like stretch of white openness so we could watch for signs of our enemies. Jake indicated that in the morning he would begin to construct what he called a fire wall—a half circle of stacked wood and branches that would surround us—to light in the event we were attacked. But we needed more loads of wood for that, so tonight we sat by one big fire—a fire that burned big and bright, a beacon for anyone—anything—wanting to find us. But our other enemy was the cold, and we had to stay warm.

It was nearly 11 o'clock before the moon rose that night. We watched it rise up from the east, an unfriendly face now partly shadowed in black.

"Don't blame the moon, Tri," Wade said. "The moon just *is*. It's not to blame for what the weren have turned themselves into."

"So Sabine Baring-Gould was wrong," I said.

"Only because he thought he had it figured out," Wade said, surprising me that he knew of the long-ago author. "But the book itself has a lot of good stuff in it."

"And so all those werewolf movies," I went on, "there was something to them after all, wasn't there? I always felt sorry for the werewolves, though. They couldn't help what they did—at least in the movies. Then in the day when they turned back to normal, they'd be scared and lonely and remorseful. Not like the vampires."

"Trust me—the Hanns—and the others like them—are not remorseful," Wade said.

"Are all werewolves like the weren?" I asked.

Wade and Jake looked at each other. "We'd always thought so, but I guess there could be other types," Wade said.

"Like in the movies," I said. "You know, there's the werewolf in *An American Werewolf in London*, then there's the werewolf in *The*

Howling and of course, all the werewolves in *Underworld*. They're kind of the same but kind of different, too."

"The Beast of Gevaudan," Wade said.

"*Le Bete*," Jake added. "Long gaping jaws, six claws."

I saw Wade smile in the firelight. "It's a werewolf story from seventeenth century France," he said. "Somewhere around a hundred people were killed over the course of three years—killed and eaten. Eventually two wolves—a male and a female pair—"

"Exceptionally large," Jake interjected.

"—were killed and the murders stopped. But over 1,000 wolves were killed first."

"Wolves are always the bad guys," Jake said. "But it's the weren. Wolves aren't evil."

"So were the 'exceptionally large' ones they killed werewolves?" I asked.

Wade shrugged. "It sounds likely, but it was a long time ago. And usually when weren die, they go back to their human form. But who knows."

"But werewolf stories, though, in general—most are probably true, aren't they?"

The brothers nodded. "The weren have been around for a long time," Wade said. "There are all kinds of stories. There's one from the fifteenth century, where a hunter was attacked by a big wolf. The hunter shot the wolf but that didn't work, and he ended up fighting it and cutting off the wolf's paw and the wolf ran away. Later, when he took the paw out of his pocket, he found a woman's hand."

"And they found the woman and burned her," Jake said.

"Was she a werewolf or was she like—like you?" I asked.

"Most people would think we *are* werewolves, Tri," Wade said. "So I don't know. She might have been just a wolf."

I wondered what people would do, now, if they knew about Wade and Jake and Su and the rest of my family. "Did your mother tell you about all this?" I asked.

"Yeah," Wade said.

"What happened to your father?"

"He left. When we were little."

"Is he like you?"

"No."

"Well, maybe he's off with my mother somewhere," I said, and we laughed a little at that. And so we passed the night, talking by the fire, and sometime well before the late winter dawn I crawled into the tent to sleep. When I woke hours later, Wade was there sleeping beside me, and in my sleep, I had inadvertently moved myself closer to his warmth. I slid away as quickly and as quietly as I could until I was out of the sleeping bag and then out of the tent. Jake glanced over at me from the fire. I joined him there, pulling on my coat and other gear. He poured some tea and handed me a warm steaming cup. My eyes scanned the distance.

"It's been quiet," he said. "But there's still awhile before moonset."

I looked at the benign looking sky. In that light blue of the early day the moon still lurked and lingered.

Awhile later I inched toward the edge and looked down the cliff. Not far from where we were was the ledge we had stood on yesterday, and down below I could see the trail Ethan and the Hanns had left behind them. Then I saw something move: a small dark wolf came into my line of vision before disappearing back up closer to the cliff and out of my sight. I rushed over to Jake.

"I saw a wolf!"

"Where?"

He followed me back to where I'd stood. We waited a few minutes, but the wolf seemed to have vanished.

Disappointed, I went back to the fire.

"It's odd," Jake said, "that it was on its own like that."

"Ethan was alone," I said.

"Ethan was on a mission."

"He was?"

"Lure the Hanns away from us. He wouldn't endanger a whole pack to do that."

"Oh." I thought about the wolf I'd just seen. What if it was Su? How would I ever know? My brief glimpse of her in wolf form was just that—a brief glimpse. But this wolf *could* be her—maybe.

A little while later Wade and Jake traded places, and I told Wade about the wolf.

"Do you think it's Su?" I asked.

He shook his head. "The pack would want her to stay. It's not likely they'd leave her alone."

I pulled a deep breath of air into my lungs. "I don't know what I'll do if she stays a wolf. I don't think I could stand it, thinking about her out here all the time, running around, maybe getting shot at by the aerial wolf hunters or maybe getting trapped. I would never know if she was alive or dead."

Wade sat with the tea kettle and a mug in hand, looking at me. "You get used to it," he said, and I remembered his mother. "But it sucks." He filled his cup. "Maybe don't worry about it now. Just keep thinking she'll come back."

"Did you ever lose Jake?"

"He's disappeared a time or two, but not for long. We're close."

"So are me and Su. At least I always thought so."

"Then she'll find you," he said.

For the first time I wondered just how close me and Su really were. Was I a good friend to her? As I thought back and remembered all the things I was always doing for her, I couldn't remember the last time we had done something fun together, just the two of us, or the last time we'd had a real heart-to-heart. Most of the time, it seemed, I was telling her what she could and couldn't do. Would she want to come back to me, or was she for once feeling free?

When Jake got up, and the moon set, we made the short trip to the cabin. While Wade and Jake loaded the sled with wood, I built a fire and melted enough snow to wash in. I did this quickly, then took a bucket of warm water outside to wash my hair. The steam swirled white in the cold. I stuck my head into the liquid warmth, then pulled it out and began to lather my hair as best I could with some old soap I'd found. As I began to rinse with one cupful of water at a time, I noticed Wade standing nearby, watching me.

"Here," he said, taking the bucket and lifting it.

"Is this a silly thing?" I asked.

"No," he said softly. "Not at all." Then he tipped the bucket and a cascade of warm wonderful water flowed over my head and down my hair.

"Thank you," I said. And I straightened and saw the gentle way he looked at me.

☽

When we returned to camp, Jake found some wolf tracks circling the perimeter. "A small one, traveling alone," he said. We all looked at them, and I thought of Su.

The Moon and the Night

Something made me look up. In the distance, in the growing dark, I saw a small canine form, which threw back its head and howled faintly into the evening. Wade and Jake looked with me, and the wolf loped away.

Nineteen

The night passed with no sign of the weren. At some point I slept. I woke up and there was Wade in the dark tent beside me. I felt how he looked at me, his face close and his fingers in my hair. I couldn't help it. I couldn't help myself and I lifted my hand and touched his cheek. He turned his lips and kissed my palm, soft and warm. Then the space between us fell away and his lips were full on mine, my arms reaching around him and pulling him close, my body protesting against the sleeping bag that separated mine from his. I shoved it away and felt him then, down the length of me, so solid and strong—

Then I felt him—Ethan—everywhere. I tried to hold onto Wade as he held onto me but then we both at once tore away from each other. The tent filled with our ragged breathing. I sat up, and Wade did the same. We watched each other in the dark.

"He won't be able to stay," Wade said.

"I think I know that."

"He shouldn't have chosen you."

And before I could ask what that meant, Wade grabbed his jacket and his boots and left.

☽

In the morning Wade kept a distance from me and Jake's eyes moved constantly from me to him. I couldn't look at him—Wade—without wanting him; I couldn't want him without longing for Ethan. My experience with boys was severely limited. I had no idea what I should do.

I concentrated on Su, calling to her in my mind. She was out there somewhere, and every day that passed took her farther and farther from ever coming back.

In the afternoon Wade and Jake's attention turned to the coming setting of the moon.

"Two-twenty-two, two twenty-two," Jake chanted at one point trying, I imagined, to lighten his brother's mood. "It's all downhill from here."

Then the magic moment arrived, and when Jake gave a whoop! and jumped up into the air, Wade had a hard time containing a smile. They surprised me by giving each other a long hug. I realized then how much they must have felt that we wouldn't make it, and I realized, too, more than ever, what they had put on the line for me this last stretch of days: each other. And that they were each other's family, each other's world.

"So what now?" I asked.

"Now," Jake said, "we figure out how *we're* going to go after *them*."

Part of me wanted to argue that, wanted to say, *Shouldn't we get out of here? Go home? Go someplace where we could get help?* But I knew I could never leave these hills without Su, and I kept my focus on that as we returned to the cabin for a break from the cold, to make some hot food, and to haul more loads of wood to add to the wooden wall we had started to build around the camp. I had looked all day for signs of the little wolf but to no avail. Still, I kept calling to her in my mind.

At our meager dinner Wade and Jake got out the map and looked at folded sections of it while we ate. "What are you looking for?" I asked.

"A crevasse, or a deep narrow gulley," Wade said. "We have to find some way to trap them." Necessity pressed him into a bit of normalcy.

"Why not just shoot them?"

"Oh, we'll do that, too," Jake added.

"We have to make sure they're mortally wounded before moonset on the day of the new moon," Wade explained, "and that they can't muster the strength to heal. Then the moon sets, and they turn human, and when the new moon rises without them, they die."

"Why not just kill them when they're human?"

"Tried that," Jake said, his mouth full. "Doesn't work."

"We don't know why," Wade added. "It's like the human part dies, but the other part comes back up with the moon. Plus it's—harder, in a different way."

I brought a spoonful of soup halfway to my mouth and froze. I heard something.

"So we're not going to do that," Wade said, searching my face.

143

"I hear something," I said. "I hear something!"

They grabbed their guns, but I got up and ran out of the cabin. I ran down the trail we had made with the snowmachine, as fast as I could, not even noticing I didn't have any boots on, only socks. "Su!" I screamed. "Su!"

And then I could see her in the dusk, a pale naked figure, trying to cover herself and spinning around frantically in her confusion. "Su!" I yelled again, and a tearful wail came from her mouth.

"Tri! Tri! Where am I? What is this? Where are my clothes?"

I grabbed her as hard as I could and held her close. Wade and Jake ran up behind me. Without saying anything Wade took off one of his shirts and I wrapped it around Su.

"Her feet," I said, seeing how white they were. "Oh, God, her feet."

At once Jake took her from me and though she screamed the whole way he ran with her in his arms, me and Wade rushing along behind.

Back inside the cabin, we placed her on the couch. "What do we do?" I asked.

"They're frostbit—bad," Wade said, and I held Su while Wade and Jake examined her feet. Soon, I knew, she would begin to scream with pain as her feet warmed—if they were still alive.

"She has to turn," Wade said, rubbing her frozen skin.

"No!" I said. "No!"

"Tri, she'll lose her feet if she doesn't. If she turns, her body can save them."

"But I just found her!"

"We'll turn with her," Wade said. "We'll turn with her, and we'll make it short."

"No—" But Wade lifted her from the couch and Jake stood ready by the door. "Just don't look, Tri, please," Wade said. "I don't want you to see me like that. Keep your gun close." Jake pulled open the door, and they crossed the threshold into the growing dark.

I tried to stay seated. I heard noises on the other side of the door. I moved cautiously toward a window and looked through a gap in the boards that covered the glass. There was a flurry of activity on the snow, like a ghostly dance in the near darkness. Then I could make out the shadowy shapes of wolves, moving now away from the cabin, a large white one looking back toward the cabin, looking back at me.

I returned to the couch and sat alone in the dim light of the cabin, afraid to move, afraid to breathe, afraid to think. It was silent outside, and dark. Where were they, and what were they doing? I felt the scar on my arm pulse. I was filled with a feeling of missing Ethan, as if I knew him better than I did, as if something more had happened between us than I'd remembered. Where was he? Did he still live?

I thought, too, of my dad, and I wondered if he never really died—if he was a wolf somewhere out here, running with a pack, living, breathing—would he remember us?

I heard wolves howling. I hoped there were only three, that more wolves didn't come to take their lost family home.

For the first time since I last walked through the door of my house nine days ago, I cried. I imagined the three of them not coming back, imagined them running off into the hills, leaving me behind. And I would be alone at moonrise, easy prey. I forced myself to shift my thoughts and concentrated on Wade and Jake bringing Su back safely and walking through the door.

Which happened, an agonizingly long hour later. Su had fainted and they carried her inside and placed her on the couch. I cradled her head in my lap and brushed back her hair. Wade took a blanket off one of the bunks and placed it over her.

"She should be okay now," Wade said. "So I guess she *was* that little wolf that was hanging around. You were right, Tri."

"I could just have easily been wrong," I said. "I had no special feeling or anything. I just hoped it might be her."

"The bond between you must be strong," Wade said. "You pulled her back."

Could that be true? My heart filled with the thought of it. I pulled the blanket up around her shoulder. "We're going to have to find her some clothes." There were drawers beneath the cubby-bed, and without needing me to ask him Wade rummaged through their contents. He found an old pair of long-johns, a sweater and some wool knickers. They would be a little big for Su but would fit her okay. He also found some pairs of wool socks and some old canvas mukluks, along with a not-very-flattering army green hat with earflaps and some big canvas mittens with wool liners. There was also an old down jacket, a little beat up but much better than nothing. I thanked Wade, then Su began to stir.

Her dark lashes fluttered, then her mismatched eyes slowly opened and looked up at me. "Tri!" she said. "I've had the weirdest dreams!" She looked around. "Why are we at the mountain cabin?"

"It's a long story, Su."

"Have I been sick?"

"Sort of."

"Why are James brothers here?" This she said in a whisper.

"They're helping us."

"Helping us what?"

"That's a long story," I said again. "Shhh. Why don't you rest some more?"

She closed her eyes. "I kept dreaming I was running through the woods," she said. "And there were wolves all over the place and I couldn't find you. And I wanted to wake up, but I couldn't. And then I heard you calling me."

She sat up, then a look of fear crossed her face and she looked quickly at me.

"What is it?" I asked.

"I don't know," she said. "Those people—"

"What people?"

"Who were in the guest cabin. What happened?"

"Do you remember?"

"No—not really."

"Then don't, Su."

"Is everything okay?"

"More or less."

I knew I couldn't keep the truth of things from Su for long, but I wanted her to have a chance to rest. "But let's get you dressed now," I said. "We've got a camp that we need to go to."

She didn't argue, but I could see all the questions she wanted to ask flitting through the expressions on her face. But for now she let them be.

When we reached camp Su immediately wanted to lie down. I took her into the cold tent and bundled her in sleeping bags.

"So when are we going home?" she asked.

"In a few days," I said, and I kissed her cheek goodnight. After some sleep she would be stronger, I reasoned, though I still didn't know how—or what—I was going to tell her.

Back outside, Wade and Jake had the fire going.

"How's she doing?" Wade asked.

"She's confused," I said.

"She will remember things."

I nodded. "Do you ever tell anyone?" I asked. "About who you really are?" I remembered the story they'd told last night, of the wolf-woman who'd been burned at the stake.

They shook their heads. "Would you?" asked Wade.

I thought of Emma and Jack. I realized that if I saw them again, I would be in the position of telling them this crazy thing or lying to them for the rest of my life.

"We kind of figured it's best not to," Wade said. "Regular people don't handle it well."

"Doesn't it make you feel lonely though? Like you're lying to all your friends?"

"We don't have many friends," Jake said.

"You must have some—some from where you used to live."

They looked at each other, and I could sense that they were communicating somehow. "We had one friend," Wade said.

"Who was that?"

"Mary. She was the only other person our age who lived out where we were. She was home-schooled, like us. Sometimes we'd get together and do things, like go sledding or ice skating."

Jake looked down at his booted feet while Wade talked.

"Mary was pretty and had these long blond braids. Her parents worked for the park service, so even though they lived way out there they had money. It was always fun to get invited to their house, like on Mary's birthday—our mom didn't exactly know how to bake a decent cake. And we met other kids at Mary's house—kids from the town. We liked being around people our own age, liked to hear stories about going to school and stuff like that. Mary was like our connection to all things normal, not to mention all things that tasted good.

"One day we were sledding down this big hill, and there was one part of it that dropped off pretty sharply—you'd be worse than hurt if you went over that edge. But our trail wasn't anywhere near it. So Mary goes to make a run, and somehow, she bounces off the path and heads right for the drop. We yelled at her to drop the sled, but she didn't. So Jake starts running, and he turns, leaping right out of his clothes.

"He caught her braids in his mouth just as she was going over and pulled her back up. But when she saw that it was a wolf that had her, she started to scream. She scared Jake so much that he turned back right there in front of her. Then she ran from us, and she never looked back. Then her dad shows up one day and tells our mother to keep us away from his daughter. I don't know what Mary told her parents, but I somehow think the bit about Jake saving her life wasn't in there.

"We liked Mary—Jake especially. But we were never invited back. Sometimes we'd see her in town when we'd go there to get supplies, and she'd act like she didn't even know us. And so we saw how it was when our true selves were seen. So we don't tell anyone."

We sat in silence for a while. Then suddenly Su screamed from the tent.

Twenty

She was flinging her arms about wildly, and I tried to grab them so they wouldn't hit my face.

"They want to hurt us! They want to hurt us!" she yelled.

"Who, Su? Who?"

"The guests! Those people! They're coming! Oh, my God they're coming!"

Then something flashed across Su's features—the wolf face, like a face beneath her face, and I saw it for only a flash of a second.

"Tri! I know they're out there!"

I thrust my head back out of the tent. Wade and Jake were dumping gas on the little wooden wall.

"She's right," Wade said, seeing me. "They're here."

A light of a match and we were encased in a half-ring of fire. "Stay here!" I said to Su and grabbed my shotgun. I hurried over to Wade and Jake. "Won't they just jump through that?" I asked.

"Weren are afraid of fire. And they're not as strong right now as they were. They'll be a lot more careful."

I tried to see beyond the fire, but the night was still pretty black, the moon rising later and later. Wade, Jake, and I formed a circle of our own, rifles raised and ready. I was suddenly aware of everything I could hear, as if my ears were turned up a few notches. The wood sizzling and popping and burning. Su's shaky breathing in the tent. And the rustling beyond the fire, the sounds of creatures pacing, breathing. I could follow them with my ears. They stood together, then apart, moving in opposite directions.

"Get Su out of the tent," Wade whispered. "Bring her out here with us."

I reached inside the tent. "Su, come out. Now."

She shook her head.

"You have to!" I grabbed Su by the arm and pulled her out. She was shaking and panting and her eyes were wild.

"She wants to turn!" Wade said when he saw her. "Don't let her! They'll tear her to pieces!"

"How do I stop it?"

"Talk to her! Slap her! Anything to keep her here!"

"Su!" I screamed. "Su! Your homework's not done! Do you hear me? Did you get Winter's coffee yet? We'll miss the bus! We'll miss the bus! Winter's still asleep! We'll miss the bus!" But still she twisted as I knelt, trying to hold her.

Then Jake was there. He grabbed Su, pulled her to him and kissed her—long and hard and romantically—and I saw her body gradually stop convulsing.

He stopped as abruptly as he'd started, then as quickly as it happened Su was looking up at me, mouth open and eyes wide.

"What—what's going on?" she stammered.

"We're being attacked," I said as calmly as I could.

"Those people—the ones in the guest cabin—"

I nodded. "But you have to stay focused, Su, you have to stay clear. Come on, get up, come stand over here with me."

We returned to the center of our area, near Wade and Jake.

Minutes crawled by. We just listened. I caught a glimpse of movement beyond the fire, pointed my gun.

"Don't shoot until they come through," Jake said. "Waste of bullets until they're close."

"Okay," I said, but the urge to start shooting was strong. I concentrated on the feeling of them out there.

"They're going to try," Wade said. "Both at once."

I listened. I heard them separate from each other; I heard them move back so they could get a running start. Then I heard something else, farther off. And a long, powerful howl broke off into the night.

Then all was movement, out there in the dark where I could not see. The weren turned away to go after other prey.

We lowered our guns and stood staring off into the dark.

"Ethan," Wade said after a while, breaking the silence. "I think they've figured out that if they come after us, he'll appear. That means every time they lose him, they'll come find us."

"That's not good," Jake said. "But maybe we can use it to trap them."

Su just stood there, taking everything in.

"Are we safe now?" I asked.

"For the time being," Wade said. "They want Ethan a whole lot more than they want us."

Su eased herself silently onto a stump by the fire, her face pale in the firelight. I stayed standing with Wade and Jake, still keeping guard. It was a while before Su said anything, but then she said this, "I was a wolf, Tri. I remember. I remember."

☽

We were on guard all through the dark of the night, but the weren never came back. We knew it was because they were now chasing Ethan. Toward dawn we let the fire border—which had melted its way deep into a trench of snow—burn itself out. Su dozed on a sleeping bag we had placed by the campfire, and I sat on stump, leaning on my shotgun for support.

"Get some sleep," Wade said. "We'll have plenty of time to see them coming."

I nodded, and lay down by Su, too tired even to crawl into the tent.

When I woke up the fire was warm and bright, and there was a warm sleeping bag covering me. It took me a moment to remember why I was sleeping outside, and then I looked up to see Su looking down at me.

"How are you feeling?" I asked.

"How would you feel if you just learned you were a freak?"

"Su—"

I sat up, and Jake handed Su a cup of tea to hand to me. It was noticeably warmer out, and my eyes took in the cloud cover that had moved in. It looked like snow, but not of the magnitude we'd had the other day. As I looked around, I saw Wade out at the fire ring, shoveling away the edges of snow where the fire had melted down into it. I looked at Jake.

"What's the plan?" I asked.

"We'll build up the fire boundary again," he said. "Then we'll just light it at moonrise. We're so close now; we need to be careful not to take any chances."

"What time is moonrise?"

"About 3:30 in the morning. But it's got to go down first."

"What time's that?"

"Moonset will occur at exactly two-twenty-one p.m.—one hour from now."

I watched Su watch Jake as he spoke. I thought about that kiss he gave her—she wouldn't easily forget that.

After moonset, we returned to the cabin. After we started a fire and Wade and Jake went outside to load the sled, Su sat down on the corduroy couch and became strangely quiet. I longed for something to say to her, the right words. But I couldn't find them.

I went outside to fill a pot of snow for water. Wade and Jake were by the woodshed, loading the sled; I could hear them talking.

Then I noticed something. The bag of Ethan's clothes, which we had kept outside by the door, was gone. I was about to yell for Wade and Jake when I turned around and saw him, a shadowy shape in the grainy fading light, standing just a short distance away.

I dropped the pot and ran.

Twenty-one

There were no words, at first. I ran into him and his arms went around me. I buried my nose in the warmth of his neck. Then he spoke quietly and hurriedly, his mouth moving near my ear. "I am so sorry, Tri—for everything that's happened. If I had known about you and Su, I never, never would have come. Look what I've done to your life—" The wind blew the snow in swirls around us. I concentrated on the feel of him, lean and warm and strong. "I'll make it right, Tri—I swear."

"Just don't go away," I said. "Don't!"

I felt him shaking his head. "I'm hunted, and the world is full of weren. It will never be safe around me."

I held him tighter, but I knew he was pulling away, knew that he would soon be gone again.

"I have to keep moving. Tell the brothers I'll be there, on the new moon. If I can come back before then without endangering all of you, I will." He released me and started walking backwards, away from me. "And tell the brothers thanks. Tell them I said thanks. I owe them—everything."

He turned and began to sprint, and I watched him gradually fade into the disappearing day. Eventually I noticed that Wade and Jake were standing wordlessly nearby. They looked at me. "He'll try to be there," I said, "on the new moon. And thanks. He says thanks."

They said nothing. I slipped back inside.

"Was that Ethan?" Su said quietly when I came in. She was looking out one of the windows, between the cracks in the boards.

"Yes."

"What did he say?"

"That he'll try to come back."

"Where did he go?"

"I don't know."

"Does he love you, Tri?"

"I don't know."

"Do you love him?"

"I don't know."

☽

Back at camp, Wade and Jake reinforced the wood wall for the barrier fire and I built up the campfire. Su said she was tired and crawled into the tent. I made myself a sitting area by the fire and sat with my shotgun across my lap, the snow swirling down from the dark sky.

Jake joined me there, after he and Wade were finished, and he sat whittling on a small piece of wood with a pocketknife. Wade remained by the exterior fire, though it was still hours until moonrise and he hadn't lit it yet.

"What's going on?" I asked.

"Wolves mate for life," he said, looking quickly at me. "That's a long time."

I looked at him.

"Just be sure about who you pick."

"I'm not 'picking' anyone."

"Tell him that," Jake said, nodding toward Wade.

I followed his gaze. Wade was kicking lightly at the stacked row of wood, as if he was making up something to keep himself busy. What would I say?

Jake was looking at me. "Don't worry too much about it right now," he said. "We've got other fish to fry."

Eventually, Wade returned gloomily to the fire where we sat around with loaded guns waiting for werewolves. But it was shortly before moonrise when we heard movement in the darkness beyond the camp.

We sat tensed with guns, then a lone howl rose up in the night, but that was quickly joined by another and another and another until the whole night was full of the longing, lonesome sound—which now completely surrounded our camp.

"Let's light it," Jake said, standing up quickly. He meant the fire ring.

"But they're just wolves, right?" I asked.

"They're after Su," Wade said as he hurried after Jake. Again they poured gas over the wood and lit it up. I stood, not knowing what to

154

do, then I noticed the walls of the tent moving strangely. Wade and Jake saw it, too.

"She's turned!" Wade said and I lunged toward the tent. "Tri! Don't go in there! She'll bite you!"

I stopped just short of the zippered entry. I could tell she was struggling to get out, and I heard snapping and snarling. In the light of the fire ring I saw the pack circling.

"They won't cross the fire," Wade said as he and Jake joined me by the tent. "But we'll have to keep it up."

"What about Su?" I asked.

"I don't know. Maybe Jake should kiss her."

"You don't—" But I saw how he was joking, and though I didn't think it was anytime to joke, I was glad to see Wade perk up a bit.

"Tent won't hold her long," Jake said.

"Will she run through the fire?"

"I hope not," Wade said. "I guess it depends how scared she is."

"What should we do?"

"Trap her," Jake said.

"What?"

"We've got some altered traps," Wade said, "from times when we had to catch our mom."

I couldn't imagine how a trap could be strong enough to hold an animal like a wolf and yet not hurt him or her.

"She'll have a sore foot—or hand," Wade said. "But she should be okay."

Jake was over at the sled, pulling a series of traps out of a canvas bag. He rushed back over, the metal contraptions dangling and clanging. He gave half to Wade, and they both started setting them by stepping on the spring lever, prying them open and pulling down the pins that held the jaws of the trap in place. They placed them in a half-circle around the front of the tent, and looped a strong rope through the rings, the ends of which Wade tied together and held tightly. Jake jumped gingerly over the ring of traps and quickly unzipped the tent and moved to the side.

The inside of the tent became quiet. Out of the corner of my eye I could see the shadows of the wolves.

Then Su came lunging out of the tent and there was the sound of one snap after another as first one front paw got caught and then, as she jerked around in fear, the other front paw landed in one of the traps, and the cold steel jaws snapped painfully shut.

Wade held fast to the rope. Su twisted and snarled and even lunged at me. Then suddenly another wolf appeared, having leapt over the ring of fire, and I found myself within feet of a large growling, snarling animal.

I held my gun, but how could I use it?

I moved to the side to put myself between the wolf and Su. It moved forward slowly, challenging me. Then as quickly as it appeared, the wolf moved backwards, turned around, and leapt back over the fire. I saw the shapes of the wolves leaving at a run.

"Moonrise," Wade said. "Damn!"

Su, now—Su the wolf—crouched down into the snow and became still. It—she—was frightened.

"Why should they chase him, when all they've got to do is come here?" Jake said, reaching for his rifle. Wade quickly tied the rope around a tree and all three of us readied our guns.

"Here we go again," Wade said.

It wasn't long before we heard the weren's throaty breathing and saw their shadowy shapes moving in and out of the firelight.

"Spread out," Jake said, motioning us to different sections of our fiery arch. I stood to the side nearest Su.

A few long moments passed when we didn't see or hear them. I saw the brothers trying desperately to pinpoint the werens' positions. I felt my skin crawling with fear. Su's wolf face twisted into a snarl, and I looked where she was looking—

I was only able to get off one shot before I was slammed into the snowy ground by a flurry of snarling fur and muscle that came spinning out of the blackness beyond the fire. Su leapt to my defense but was tossed aside with one swipe of a clawed hand. I felt a crushing pressure on my shoulder and braced myself. As the brothers rushed to me a great silver gray and white wolf leapt into our circle, charged at the weren pinning me down and then lunged away at a run.

But the weren didn't follow.

"They're trapping him!" Wade shouted.

They couldn't shoot out of fear of hitting me. They pulled long lengths of wood from the fire and shoved them at the weren, lighting its fur. The wolf that was Ethan ran in circles, trying to get the weren to follow him.

"Go!" I heard Wade shout to Ethan. "Go!"

How Ethan understood I don't know, but the wolf made one last pass then raced away, leaping over the fire and into the darkness where the other weren waited.

We were left to fight. Its flaming fur forced the weren to spin off me and roll its back into the snow before leaping up and out of our camp, the volley from Wade and Jake's rifles ringing through the blackness of the early November morning.

Wade then fell to his knees beside me and hurriedly pulled back my coat and sweater to look at my shoulder. His face looked frantic, then it calmed. "I'd say you were lucky, but luck had nothing to do with it," he said, his relief evident. "They didn't want to kill you, or you would be dead. And they didn't want to turn you, either—they were careful not to break the skin." Then his face looked shadowed. "I think they've figured out they can use you to trap Ethan. Biting you was just for show."

As Jake joined his brother in examining my shoulder, I saw Su writhing in the snow nearby. "It's okay—she's turning," Wade said quickly, and Jake took off his coat and threw it over Su then quickly freed her paws from the traps.

Wade gently touched my skin. "You'll be sore for a while, Tri, but that's it—nothing's going to happen." As he said it, I began to imagine what we—what I—would be facing if the weren had broken skin with its venomous teeth.

"Tri!"

I looked over at Su—who was now really Su again—wrapped in Jake's coat and looking at me with wide, frightened eyes.

"I'm okay," I said. "Are you?"

She nodded but said, "My hands hurt." I could tell, though, as she flexed them, that they were okay.

"Go get dressed," I said, looking toward the tent. "I'm fine."

Su looked down at herself, confused again, but hurried into the tent.

"Let's get you by the fire," Wade said, and he helped me up. Jake was heating water, and soon both he and Wade were fussing over my shoulder as they cleaned it and checked again for breaks in the skin. Su came out of the tent and sat quiet and close. Jake made a pot of tea, and we talked little as we waited for the rest of the dark morning to pass.

I fell asleep a little after daylight broke and awoke to more cloudy skies. Wade and Jake were still keeping guard; Su, I assumed, had gone off to sleep in the tent.

"Hi," Wade said when he saw my open eyes. "How's the shoulder?"

"Sore," I said, wincing as I tried to move it. "But okay."

Jake poured me some tea, but I could tell the brothers were reluctant to take too much attention off the area surrounding the camp.

"We're going to go to the ledge tonight," Wade said. "Even though their power's diminishing, the Hanns are stepping up their game. On the ledge there's only one way they can come for us."

"The moon will come up around five in the morning," Jake added. "Sun will come up three or four hours after that, so we won't have to deal with darkness and the weren for too long."

"Can Su shoot?" Wade asked.

"A little. I mean, she's fired a rifle before and knows how to use one. Why?"

"We might need her to. We've got to wait it out a few more days but then we've got to give it to them."

"I just don't see how they'd be that stupid to give us that opportunity," I said.

"Well," Jake said, "we're going to have to trick them, and we're going to have to make it good."

We stayed at camp after moonset, and Wade and Jake slept while Su and I kept guard. I knew Su was confused still, and afraid; I wished so badly that there was something I could do to make it better for her.

"Tri," she said quietly. "What if Winter's dead?" Her big eyes met mine, the blue and the brown.

"We'd get by, Su," I said. "Tabby would probably come live with us until I turned eighteen, and then we could just be on our own."

"You can't even drive!"

"Well, I will. I'll get my license."

Su's eyes wandered away from mine. "Would Ethan stay with us?"

I hesitated, then said, "I don't think he can stay, Su. All this—is about him, you know."

"Where will he go?"

"I don't know, Su."

"So we'll just—go back to normal? I mean, providing Winter's okay."

I nodded, but I didn't think anything would ever be normal again.

Hours later we were moving through the dark, leaving our beloved warm fire behind. With Jake in the lead and Wade in the rear, we walked closely together. No moon yet and cloudy skies made for a lot of darkness. Even though we didn't have to worry about the weren— for the moment—Wade and Jake, I knew, were concerned the Hanns would attempt to do what they could in their human form.

When we got below the ledge, we had to start climbing. Wade and Jake turned on their headlamps, though I knew they didn't want to. I stayed in back of Su, hoping I could catch her if she fell.

Jake reached the ledge first and reached down to help Su then me over the lip. Wade followed, and we sat down on some sleeping bags that we had carried with us. We also brought water, a thermos of tea and the usual barrage of firearms. So it was sit and wait. There was a slim chance, of course, that the weren could leap down from above and somehow land on the ledge, but it was unlikely. "They're not smart enough to calculate that right," Wade said. "The *Hanns* may be, but when they turn the brawn becomes greater than the brain."

As it got closer to moonrise we quit talking and just sat there, Su and I together and Wade on my side with Jake on hers. Su holding a gun made me a little nervous, and I found myself lightly slapping her hand each time I caught her fidgeting anywhere near the trigger. She would glare defiantly at me when I did so, and I tried to soften it all with smiles in the dark but these she quickly looked away from.

Moonrise was at 4:56 that dark morning and we waited, barely breathing, for nearly an hour before we sensed movement below. Jake stretched his arms across the front of us and signaled for us to stand and get our rifles ready. They were following our upward trail. Jake motioned to Wade and on the count of two they both turned their headlamps on, and light spilled down on the two dark forms working their way up the steep face. The weren swung their monstrous heads at the light but kept coming, noticeably slower than their attempted ascent just days previous. At Jake's signal we fired: sharp, crackling sounds reverberating through the night. The creatures fell backward and tumbled out of sight.

I lowered my gun and at the same time grabbed my bruised shoulder, my face twisting against the pain.

"Forget something?" Wade whispered and I nodded. Everything grew quiet again. The brothers swept the areas below us with their headlamps.

"They're recovering," Jake said. "We've probably got a good half hour before the next attack."

We waited. A half hour turned into an hour, then an hour and a half. Then we heard a long, low, gruesome howl rise up from the darkness. It was joined by another. Su dropped her gun and clasped her hands over her ears; I fought an urge to do the same.

"What's happening?" I said.

"Well," Jake replied. "I guess they decided to try something else."

Before I could ask what, I felt Wade shaking beside me and Su fell down on her knees.

Jake looked sharply at his brother. "Don't turn!" he hissed. "Don't you fucking turn!"

"I won't!" Wade said. "I won't!" But his voice had a strain in it that I had never heard before. I sensed his struggle.

"Su," I said. "Su! Stop it!" But her hands were over her ears, and her head was down between her knees. I noticed Jake breathing strangely.

Oh, God—I sized up my situation. If they turned there were two things that would happen: they would either flee down the face to certain doom, or stay here on the ledge with me, acting who knows how. Of course I prayed for the latter. But either way left one gun to fire down upon the Hanns.

"Tri," Jake said, his breathing pant-like. "Don't let us go down that slope. Shoot us if we do."

"What?"

"Shoot us. You'll have to be fast, and your aim will have to be sharp."

"I can't do that. I can't!"

"You've no idea what they'll do us, Tri. No idea—Wade!" he shouted. "Pull out of it! Now!"

But Wade was twisting on the narrow ledge. Su was shaking her head around and moaning.

"Damn it!" Jake said. He pushed past me and to my horror he hit Wade over the head—hard—with the butt of his rifle.

A scream stuck in my throat. Down below the awful howling continued. Suddenly Jake lurched onto the floor of the ledge beside his now-still brother. Strange sounds were coming from everywhere—cracking, popping sounds. Then I noticed the howling was getting closer.

"Oh God!" I said. "Oh God!" I snatched the headlamp off Jake's churning head and put it on. The light shone down the slope. They were coming again. I pumped shells into the chamber and shot. They kept coming. I kept shooting.

Then suddenly snow fell on me from up above. And before I could comprehend what might be happening now, a figure came swinging down, landing on the ledge beside me. Ethan. It was Ethan.

He scooped up a gun.

"We do this together," he said.

I looked at him and tried to breathe. The light from the headlamp swept across his face and my eyes locked with his.

"From now on, we do this together." And he lifted his gun.

Twenty-two

We sent volley after volley of bullets flying down the slope. When one rifle emptied, we grabbed another and used that. Finally they fell backwards, the light from the headlamp revealing streaks of blood in the snow.

"Reload," Ethan said, and we grabbed bullets and slipped them into magazines. "Pull her up," Ethan said, motioning to Su.

I grabbed her and yanked her to her feet; she struggled wildly against me. Ethan grabbed Jake and was in the process of raising him when suddenly he said, "They're coming," and we dropped them both and went back to firing.

"They're hurt," he said. "They need to rest." But on they came, desperate to get us.

Then I saw we shared the ledge with three wolves, struggling out of human clothes.

"Keep firing!" Ethan said to me, and he grabbed Wade—or Jake—as one or the other of them made a dash for the edge. The wolf snapped and snarled but Ethan managed to get a hold of it and threw it up against the rock wall where it lingered only a moment before lunging forward again. Ethan stuck out his arm and caught it—somehow—by the snout, gripping the wolf's jaws closed. He then locked eyes with the wolf, released it and the animal backed away.

The same scenario replayed with the other large wolf, but the wolf that was Su—I noticed as I tried to keep track of what was happening both and on and below the ledge—was in effect hiding in the shadows behind us.

Ethan rejoined me. A few more shots and the Hanns were knocked back again, this time obviously wounded and bleeding fiercely.

Ethan looked at me. Behind us came the strange sounds of wolves turning back into humans. In the distance, the first hint of gray light was breaking through the dark.

We watched the dawn together—all five of us, waiting for what the slow emerging light would reveal, and after nearly an hour we could discern blood and tufts of fur on the torn-up slope, but the Hanns had disappeared.

Jake looked at his watch. "Five and a half hours left."

"That's enough," Ethan said, "for them to heal and regroup. But they won't like the light. They won't come at us this way." He looked above us. "They'll see my tracks. They might try it."

Ethan was thinking; so was Jake. Wade came up close to my side. Our eyes met. I wanted to tell him it was okay. There was a gash on his forehead where Jake had hit him with the gun. I lifted my hand to touch it, but he turned away.

Ethan and Jake spoke quietly. We would go back to camp, traveling along the side of the slope until we could find a place where we could safely crest. We gathered up what we'd brought with us, then we moved single file off the ledge and made our way slowly forward, sinking into the snow and fighting gravity.

Eventually we came to a spot where we could see over the crest of the slope enough to discern that the Hanns weren't in the immediate area. We climbed up cautiously at first, then quickly. We found our trail and hiked hurriedly back to camp, guns ready, but still there was no sign.

We built a fire, and Su soon crawled off to bed, saying to wake her up if something bad started happening. We were all tired, but moonset was still not until after two in the afternoon.

Ethan and Jake spoke quietly just beyond the campfire and Wade and I sat there, watching the horizon. Finally Wade broke the silence.

"You know I love you, Tri," he said, his voice quiet. "From the moment I saw you." He didn't look at me as he spoke.

"I think I do know that."

"And you have feelings for me, too. I've felt them."

"Yes."

"But there's Ethan."

"Yes."

"He'll have to leave, Tri."

I nodded. "I know that."

"But I'll still be here when he does." He let himself look at me for a brief moment. Then Ethan and Jake joined us at the fire. Ethan squatted down next to me, looking in my eyes. I felt Wade bristle beside me.

"We have an idea," Ethan said quietly. "But I need to ask you to do something."

There was a plan. A trap. Together Ethan and I would be the bait; we would be on one side of a crevasse, and the others would be on the other side. When the weren came for me and Ethan, we would leap the crevasse and Wade, Jake, and Su would shoot the weren as they followed. I agreed. We were essentially bait already. But I had no idea how I was supposed to leap a crevasse.

Wade looked at his brother. Something passed between them. Then Wade stood abruptly and walked off to the edge of the camp.

"At moonset, Jake and I will check out possible sites," Ethan said. "We'll go in wolf form, and we won't be gone long." Ethan rose and found a place to sit a little distance from the fire. A little distance from me. And Wade stayed away.

Moonset came, and Ethan and Jake disappeared behind the trees. A few minutes later two large, beautiful wolves emerged and ran out of the camp. I watched them disappear into the white distance. After a time Wade returned to the campfire.

"You can get some sleep," Wade said. "I've got this." He looked down at the snowy ground, then let his eyes meet mine.

"I don't know what's going to happen, Wade."

"None of us do." He tore his eyes away from mine. "So let's not worry about anything we don't have to. And you should get some sleep."

"I'll keep you company," I said, but as I began to relax I felt myself getting sleepier and sleepier, absorbing the heat from the fire. I finally sank down on a sleeping bag, still intending to stay awake, but sleep soon overtook me.

When I woke up, I thought at first that I had only dozed off for ten or fifteen minutes, but as my head cleared and I took everything in I saw that Wade's typical sitting place was empty, and I looked across the fire and saw Ethan's face through a swirl of smoke, his dark eyes watching me.

We stared at each other. I felt my heart pump and my breathing quicken. I felt a tingling sensation and an overwhelming urge to leap across the flames and touch him, feel him, kiss his lips and bury my hands in his dark hair. I had a vision then, of the two of us: in the snow, his mouth on mine, a feeling of being one, a feeling of always having been. I let myself sink into it, his eyes still fast on mine. Did he feel it, too? Was this what it was to love?

Then I became aware of the movements of others: Jake, Su, Wade but Wade keeping his distance from Ethan, from me. I held Ethan's eyes for a final few moments. I knew something, then: he and I were connected, in a way I felt but didn't understand.

☽

Moonrise came at 6:30 the next morning. The night had passed quietly but not without tension: Ethan had paced restlessly near the outskirts of the camp, Wade skulked wherever Ethan wasn't, and Jake and I made tea and food and tried our best to distract an increasingly pale and nervous Su.

"They're growing weaker all the time," Jake had told her as she worried about the weren. "Soon it will be piece of cake, taking them down."

"But what if we don't?" Su had asked.

"We will."

"How do you know?"

"Because Wade and I have done this before," Jake had said. "This is what we do."

He'd smiled at her. She'd smiled back but then her eyes searched out Ethan in the dark.

So moonrise that dark cold morning found us un-rested and agitated, but ready with rifles and a replenished fire ring. Ethan continued to pace, tilting his face up into the wind. "What if they don't show?" I asked Jake.

"Then they're smarter than we thought."

Hours passed. Then we heard something coming—a soft and padded sound, almost inaudible. Wade and Jake turned on their headlamps. A large pack of wolves was gathering around us.

"What are they doing?" I looked hurriedly at Su, who stared mesmerized at the animals.

"Visiting," Jake said, his voice hushed. "They mean no harm."

"But Su—"

"I've got her," Jake said. I saw how his hand rested on her shoulder as she sat, how her own arm was wrapped tightly around his leg.

Wade came closer and stood by me. "They're the ones who

followed us," he said, "from the second camp."

I could see the great black wolf that had run along beside me.

"So if they're here, does that mean the weren aren't?" I whispered. Wade and Jake nodded. Light was beginning to leak into the darkness. I could make out Ethan near the fire ring. Then he stepped over it, and the wolves surrounded him. I jolted forward but Wade's arm stopped me. "They want him to run with them," he said. "It's all right."

I watched him walk among them, graceful and at ease, then Ethan and the wolves faded into the grainy gray of the morning.

☽

Ethan came back in the early afternoon, and no one said anything as he sat down by the fire. Jake handed him some tea, and he whispered a thank you. After a moment of silence Jake asked, "Any sign of them?"

Ethan shook his head. He took a sip from his tea before saying, "I think they want us to think they're gone."

"Do we think they're gone?"

Ethan looked at him. "Do you?"

"Hell no."

"I agree."

"But why would they do that?" Su asked.

"So we'd let our guard down," Wade said.

"But we won't do that," Su said.

"But we'll let them think we have," Jake said.

"How?"

"We've got that figured out."

And I saw how Wade looked at me, and how Su saw his face. "Tri," she said. "What's going on?"

☽

There was a somberness over the camp that night: Ethan paced silently, the brothers were of few words, and Su and I sat quietly and close to each other. I knew she was worried, and scared. Of all the things to worry about I worried most about being separated from her.

Su and I slept for a few hours in the tent; I think each of us was hoping to escape into happy dreams. I fell asleep thinking thoughts of home, and I dreamt of the entryway and Ethan. He pressed himself against me, whispered my name. Then he said, *Go to him, Trileka...*

I shook my head, I tried to cry out, *Please don't leave*—but I woke up and there was Su, crying and twitching in her sleep. "Su," I said, "wake up—you're dreaming!"

She opened her eyes and blinked at me in the dark. "You're dreaming," I said again.

She sat up and pushed her hair out of her face. She looked older, suddenly, like she was now growing up at an accelerated pace. "It seemed so real," she said. "It was like it was *real*." She looked at me. "Tri," she said.

I shook my head. "It was just a dream." I stroked her shaking back, wondering what dark thoughts had found her in her sleep.

"Hey, Tri." Wade's voice came softly from outside the tent. "Moonrise."

"Okay." I said.

"I'm coming, too," Su said. We slipped on our boots and coats and joined the others at the campfire in the morning darkness for another cold wait.

But nothing happened. Nothing—no weren, no wolves. I could see how the inaction disturbed Wade, Jake, and Ethan, even though it could aid in our final plan. But I began to think they worried the Hanns really did leave.

"Tomorrow," Ethan said as daylight began to creep over the horizon. "Tomorrow we'll know."

We didn't wait until moonset to pack the camp and make the trip down to the cabin. We would need every hour after that to travel. It was another gray day, and while the light snow that was falling would not be enough to complicate our plans, it was enough to coat everything with a sense of gloom. As we approached the cabin, Ethan and Jake went up ahead and made sure there were no surprises there, and we were all careful to keep a look out as we made our final preparations to part. Su would go with Wade and Jake. Ethan and I would head out on our own.

Su and I went inside the quiet cabin for one last look.

"Su," I said. "It could be that nothing will even happen tomorrow."

"But wouldn't that just make everything worse?"

She was right and I had no response. We would have to go through this all over again.

"I just want to go home," she said. "I want this to be over, and I want us to go home." Her lips trembled a little, but she did not cry.

"It's going to be okay, Su," I said.

"No, it's not!"

"Yes, it is."

"It's not, Tri, I saw it!"

"You mean in your dream?"

"It was more than a dream, Tri." She looked at me. "I saw it, the crevasse, everything. And you fell. You fell with one of them and went right over the edge!"

I swallowed, and tried to manage a smile despite a sinking feeling in my heart. "It was a dream, Su, that's all. Of course you're worried. I'm worried, too. But we have to keep thinking we'll make it home—all of us. We have to keep thinking that."

"I would miss you so much, Tri." She looked away as she spoke, and I saw how she struggled for control.

"I won't fall, Su."

But I knew that might not be up to me.

A short time later we were saying our goodbyes in front of the cabin door. Su clung to me for a long moment before climbing onto the snowmachine behind Jake. Wade stepped close and met my eyes. "We'll take care of Su," he said. He touched the side of my face. I felt a tightening in my throat. Would I ever see him again? "Yes," he whispered and reluctantly pulled back his hand and tore his eyes away from mine. He got on the machine behind Su, looked at Ethan, then back at me, and then they were gone.

Ethan and I watched the snowmachine until it was out of sight. Then we turned on our snowshoes and walked off into the silence and the snow.

Twenty-three

I walked gloomily behind Ethan, our snowshoes leaving a woven trail behind us. The miles stretched out as we went deeper into the wilderness, closer to the unknown of tomorrow. My heart was hopeful and heavy at once. We might succeed. We might not. Maybe we go home, and maybe we don't go home again, ever.

I tried to keep pace with Ethan, but it was hard. Now and again he stopped and waited for me to catch up. We were trying to get as far as we could before we lost the light; we did have one of the brothers' headlamps, which would help, but the deep wilderness such as what we were in takes on an extra weight after dark. It was better to see. Better not to wonder at the shadows and shapes.

The light was getting gray and grainy when I felt how we were heading upwards. Trees appeared here and there, solitary sentries in this lonely snow-washed world. It was a place where you expected to see ghosts—lost hunters, lost travelers, missing pilots like my dad, spirits wandering the wilderness, unable to find a way out. As if having to worry about werewolves wasn't enough.

The trees began to thicken, and it became more difficult to see. Ethan remained a dark shape in front of me, and I kept my eye on him as best I could. At one point he stopped, and I caught up with him.

"Are you doing okay?" he asked. Even in the dark I could see how handsome he was, his dark eyes bright and alert, his thick dark hair framing his narrow face.

"Yes," I said.

"We can take a break if you want."

"I'd rather keep going," I said. I knew he would not want—not need—to stop.

He nodded, then said, "I'm going to get you home, Tri. I promise."

The air felt magnetic between us. He turned abruptly and started walking.

About an hour later we came out of the trees. Ethan walked a short stretch farther then stopped. I came up along beside him.

"The crevasse is there," he said, pointing to the blackness in front of us.

My eyes strained against the dark, trying to see it.

"It's not very wide here—eight feet or so," Ethan said.

I nodded, a sick feeling swirling in my stomach.

"You'll make it, Tri. You're stronger than you know."

I looked at him and found his eyes in the dark. I felt something pass between us. We were not normal. An image of my dreams flashed through my mind. Running, leaping, a feeling of power.

"We'll camp here," Ethan said, and I followed his lead and took off my pack, setting it upright in the snow. I watched as he stomped down a spot with his snowshoes, then I followed him back into the woods and we broke dead branches off the spruce trees and cut some small, standing dead trees for a fire, wordlessly working together but carefully keeping a physical distance. If he touched me now I wasn't sure I would know where to stop, and somehow I knew he felt this, too.

Later, with the fire going, we kept the burning wood between us, and after I couldn't stand it any longer, I broke the silence.

"What was your life like, before you came here?" I asked.

His eyes were on the flames. "Sometimes it was normal, sometimes not."

"Where did you live?"

"My mother and I moved a lot."

"How did your father die?"

"They said it was a motorcycle accident. But it was weren."

"I'm sorry."

"It happened before I was born." His eyes met mine through the smoke of the fire.

I felt a sense of time running out, of rushing forward. "What are your dreams?"

"My dreams?"

"Beyond this. Beyond surviving. If you could be—normal."

"I'd live in a city," he said, his voice softening. A slight smile crossed his face. "With bookstores and music shops and movie theatres. In an apartment that looked down on a busy street."

I let his words take my mind there, then, and I saw him: a busy sidewalk, awash with people, Ethan among them, smiling. Just another person, one among many.

"That's not so big a dream," I said.

"No. And your dreams?"

"I've always only wanted to be a historian. I don't know why. I like seeing the history in things—it's like one big story that goes on and on and on."

His eyes held mine through the sparks and the smoke. My heart was pounding, my blood pulsing.

"I want you to have your life," he said. "If I had known about you, I would never have come here. I just want to get you home, you and Su."

"I want you to get home, too—"

"I won't be able to stay."

"I don't want you to leave."

"I can't stay."

"Then let me go with you." I surprised myself with those words.

"Tri, it will never be safe around me. Never."

"So I'm supposed to forget you?"

"Yes."

"I won't be able to."

"You have to."

He rubbed his forehead. Was he shaking? With a sudden rush of courage I moved to the other side of the fire and touched his trembling wrist.

"Are you all right?"

"Tri, don't get so close."

"What is it?"

"You." He lifted his eyes toward mine. "Don't get so close. Please."

I felt my insides shake. There was so much I longed to say, but my lips only trembled.

My whole life I never felt I could have anything I wanted, really wanted. I never felt like anything ever really belonged to me.

"I can't stay with you, Tri. It would be wrong—to start something, and then have me leave."

And now I see how much I do have. And now I see how wonderful life is. And now I see it's you, Ethan, it's all because of you—

I was on my knees in the snow beside him. My heart felt huge in my chest, huge and full where it pounded against muscle and bone, a knocking. I took short, quick breaths and willed myself to speak. "This is my story," I said finally, my voice quiet and shaky. "My history. I don't want this part to not be there." I wanted my story. My story that belonged to only me—

We looked at each other. I could feel the silent communication between us: this was how it was supposed to be, this moment, this now. Then he reached out and touched the side of my face, and I drew a sharp breath as a current of sensation seared through me. All at once he kissed me, his hands knocking my hat off and roaming through my hair, his mouth fierce and warm. Then he pulled his lips away from mine, kissed the side of my face and held me in a tight embrace, his body shaking. I pulled him to me as tight as I could and gradually felt his breathing steady. He kissed my face again then pressed his forehead against mine, our cold noses touching each other in the space between.

"I want to be with you, Tri," he said, his voice quiet. "More than you could imagine. I want to be with you in every way possible, but I can't—we can't. I won't be able to be with you, Tri."

"Then be with me now. Here."

"Tri—" he whispered. "Trileka. I can't be that part of your story. That would bond you to me forever—for the rest of your life, and you need to have a good life—you deserve to be able to make that story wonderful. And I need—I need to be able to think of you, Tri, to see you in my mind living a life I can't—going to college, going out with people, having friends, and having fun. Just—walking down a street somewhere, living a life."

"I don't want a life without you, Ethan."

"Then take me with you into yours—I will be able to *feel* you, Tri, no matter how great the distance. I'll feel your joy, and I'll feel your pain—so let there be a lot of happiness, Tri. Let your laughter find me, like the wind in the trees."

"I'll take you with me," I said, my voice a whisper. "But be with me now."

"Tri—"

"Can't you see everything's already happened between us?"

"Tri, wolves—"

"I know," I whispered. "I know."

He closed his eyes. After a moment he opened them, so close to mine our lashes fluttered together, like tiny wings. Our eyes locked, and I felt something pulling from deep down inside of me, something as ancient as the glaciers and as wild as a winter night. My hands roamed his hair and our faces moved together, forehead to forehead, nose to nose, then his lips pressed against my parted lips, lightly at first, his breathing deep but steadier now, and he kissed my lower lip, my upper lip, my cheek, my chin, my neck. I put my arms around him as he continued to kiss me, each touch of his lips reaching down beneath my skin, touching all that I ever was, all that I ever would be, and all that I am. The history of me.

☽

When I woke up, it was light. The space where Ethan had slept beside me was empty. I sat up and found him, standing by the edge of the crevasse. He looked over his shoulder and saw that I was awake. I watched him walk toward me, a strange squeezing on my heart. He knelt down in the snow and touched his forehead to mine.

"Trileka Tyler," he whispered.

"Is it time yet?" I held the collar of his coat, keeping him close.

"No, not yet. Are you all right?"

"Yes."

"We'll make it through this. And then you'll be home."

"And then you'll be gone."

I heard the intake of his breath. *I will never leave you, Tri.* I felt the words, as clearly as if he'd spoken out loud. But already I could feel his impending absence, and with that came a yearning, a longing, a feeling of wanting to throw my head back and wail at the fathomless sky.

His warm hand touched my cheek. "Come here," he said. "Come with me for a moment." He pulled me up and I stepped out of the sleeping bag. I slipped on my boots, and he took me down the path he'd made with his snowshoes to the edge of the crevasse. "Look," he said.

"I don't want to."

"Just look at it, Tri. Look at where you are right now and look where you'll need to get to. Don't worry about what's beneath you. Don't worry about you're going to do it. Just look at that other side, and picture yourself over there, safe." I did what he said, only I imagined myself sailing over the distance between where we were and the other side, like a bird.

We waited, sitting close on top of the sleeping bags in the snow.

173

Quietly together, our arms wrapping, our hands caressing. Hearts pulsing, beating away the minutes like twin clocks.

Then Ethan's face became more alert, and he looked in the direction of the trees. A flock of chickadees flew out of the woods and over the crevasse to the other side. A half dozen ptarmigan then flew up out of the snow nearby, feathers as white as angels' wings, their flight as silent as a ghost's.

I looked at Ethan. "They're coming," he said, and he stood and took my hand, helping me to me feet. My legs felt weak and trembling.

"Wait," I said, and strapped my father's shotgun across my chest. Then Ethan led me down the trail he had made, stopped several yards short of the edge, and looked at me.

"It's all right," he whispered. And he ran his fingers lightly over the side of my face. Despite my growing fear I felt that touch, all through my being. His fingers moved slowly to the back of my neck, and he brushed my hair back from my face. Then he put his face close to mine and touched my nose with his. "This is real," he whispered. "This is real. From the first moment I saw you I knew you were my family. My home. Remember that I love you, Trileka Tyler."

And for a moment when his lips fell on mine there was nothing but that kiss, nothing but the taste of him, the smell of him, the feel of him flooding into me. For a moment. Then suddenly he said:

"Run!"

He grabbed my hand as I saw, in what felt like slow motion, the weren leaping out from the trees with their snapping and snarling and foaming jaws and we rushed forward toward the crevasse and before I could say, before I could think, *I can't do this*, we were leaping in the air and falling into the snow on the other side.

"Stay down!" Ethan said and a volley of gunshots cracked through the morning. Then something came down on us and I was tossed upward. I scrambled to my feet and swung my father's shotgun forward. The weren's great jaw was open and coming down on Ethan's neck. I put my shotgun near the side of its face and fired. It released Ethan, wobbled and grabbed me, and as it fell backwards I was pulled with it, over the edge and into the air.

Survivors of car accidents are known to say that time slowed as they saw themselves heading for disaster. I felt myself in the air, spinning, falling. I thought of my family; I thought of my father and felt him there with me. *Hang tight, Tri. Hang tight.* The bottom of the crevasse came closer and closer—

I looked up and saw Ethan falling, flying through the air, coming for me.

☽

I remember a few things: the world shifting beneath me, then rising and discarding me. Ethan, untangling my father's gun from my battered body, shots echoing around me. The knowledge that he was hurt and bleeding. The feel of falling into the snow as my head filled with soft white clouds.

I don't know where I went, but I felt as if I was gone.

And then there was a voice, saying my name: *Trileka. Tri. Wake up, Tri, wake up.* I felt myself swimming through fog, rushing to the surface and slowly I opened my eyes.

I saw a face. Round and open. A face I knew. "Wade," I whispered.

"Shhh, Tri, it's all right. Don't talk."

I tried to sit up, but he gently eased me back down.

"Su—"

"She's all right. Jake's with her."

"Ethan."

He didn't answer. I said again, "Ethan."

"We don't know. He's wounded. He's with the wolves."

I tried to look around. There was sky above me. The sides of cliffs. The crevasse. I was in the crevasse. "The weren," I said. Again I tried to sit.

"Don't look," Wade said. "Don't."

But I had seen a woman's body, bloody in the snow. Long blond hair. I heard the accent in my memory: Mrs. Hanns. And the body of a man, half buried.

I felt myself shaking. Wade's warm hands cupped my face, his white-blue eyes holding mine. "Don't," he whispered. "Don't, Tri. Just breathe. It's okay. Breathe and stay still. We'll get you out of here."

I felt hot tears sliding free and falling down my cheeks. Wade gently wiped them away. "You were so brave," he said. "And you were so beautiful, jumping that crevasse."

I reached up for him, then drifted away.

I heard my name, again. And again I came back.

After a time Wade propped me up in the snow and fed me some water, carefully spooning it into my mouth. I moved my eyes. I didn't see the bodies, though there was plenty of blood on the snow around us.

"What happened?" I asked.

"The Hanns—the weren—are dead. But we have to wait until the new moon rises without them. Then they'll be gone."

"But what happened?" I asked again.

"One of them took you with it when it fell. Ethan jumped after you. You landed on the weren, but neither of them was dead. Ethan shot them with your shotgun, and Jake and I hit them from above with our rifles. Eventually they went down. But Ethan was hurt, and all these wolves came down the canyon and carried him away. It didn't seem real. But it was beautiful."

"Will he live?"

"We don't know."

Again there was a squeezing on my heart.

I felt my strength returning, a little bit at a time. The day started fading and Wade built a fire. Suddenly I realized that Jake and Su were right above us, on top of that sheer wall. They threw sleeping bags down to us which Wade wrapped around me. As the day turned to night he sat close, a rifle across his lap.

"Stay awake as long as you can," he said. "You might have hit your head. You should stay awake."

"All right. I'll try."

"It seems like we'll be going home," he said. "The moon is new at about eight o'clock tomorrow morning. When it comes up at eleven, we're home free."

I tried to imagine that. "Tomorrow's Thanksgiving," I said.

"Happy Thanksgiving, Tri."

"Happy Thanksgiving, Wade." But somewhere out there in the dark, Ethan struggled.

And so Thanksgiving morning dawned, and at exactly 11:02 a.m. Wade proclaimed that the Hanns were no longer. He buried the bodies in the snow and Jake tossed snowshoes down to us.

"Are you strong enough to walk?" Wade asked. Slowly he helped me to my feet. I nodded and stood like a little girl as he strapped the snowshoes onto my boots.

We traveled down the canyon, searching for a place where we could climb out. It was hours before we found a good enough spot, and when we came up over the edge Su and Jake were there to meet us. Su flung herself around me and cried. Then we built a fire and made tea and ate a portion of what little food we had left. And we waited for sign of Ethan.

Late that afternoon we heard wolves howling, and for the first time in what seemed a lifetime it was a happy sound for me. I knew what it meant. They were bringing him back. And then I saw him, walking along the edge of the trees, Ethan. Coming back. Coming back to me.

Epilogue

Winter, Su, Sydney, Tabby, and I sat with Wade at the ceremony, serving as the family he didn't have, as we watched Jake walk with the other graduates at River Valley High. The events of the winter were long behind us now, but each of us carried with us our own scars, some visible, some not. And I said a prayer every night. For Ethan. Wherever he was.

It was only two days after we got back that I went out to the guest cabin and found he was gone. That I would ever see him again was unknown and probably unlikely. But every day I hoped.

I tried to keep all that from Wade, but he knew. He wasn't stupid.

But the scar on my arm, which seemed to beat with my very heart, was always there to remind me. Not that I could ever forget. And in addition to the prayer I said each night for Ethan, I said a prayer of thanks each morning when I opened my eyes to another day in history.

So far I had not turned, or showed any signs that I would. And Su was learning to control her own malady.

There had been a half-hearted search for the missing Hanns and a few newspaper articles. The Hanns themselves had completely covered their own tracks, making sure there was no connection with us. When their dog team was "found" not far from Susitna Station (Winter had kept the dogs with her and later planted them where they would be spotted), there was a brief search in our area. But then a pile of human bones was found in the Hanns' Merlin River residence, and they were sought for a different reason. But hopefully they'll never be found. Su and I kept the dog team, as no one came forward to claim it, and the dogs grew happier with each passing day.

We let Dangerous Dan adopt two of them, though only Wade and Jake and I knew why.

Now, at Jake's graduation, we watched him traipse across the gymnasium stage in his royal blue gown, grinning from ear to ear. Not bad for someone raised by a wolf. Then the ceremony was done, the graduates threw their caps into the air, and we stood and clapped and cheered. I felt a hand on my shoulder.

I turned and saw Mr. Palmer. "Another day in history, eh, Tri?"

I smiled. And so it was. Yet I wondered, now, at all the history out there which lay buried like the Hanns in the snow, hidden like the truth about the scars on my arm.

Or which was kept safe, and silent, in the secret hearts of lovers.

Acknowledgements

Many thanks to Whitney Wolfe, who helped me create the character of Winter Wolfe, the original inspiration for this story. *The Encyclopedia of Vampires, Werewolves and Other Monsters* by Rosemary Guiley was an important resource in the writing of this book, as was *The Book of Werewolves: Being an Account of a Terrible Superstition* by Sabine Barring-Gould.
Wolf paw and moon phase artwork by CreativeRiotDesign, Sweden.

About the author

Sarah Birdsall has lived in Alaska most of her life, with many of her formative years spent in remote parts of the state. She is the author of the award-winning novels, *Wild Rivers, Wild Rose* and *The Red Mitten*. A former award-winning journalist, she has an MFA in creative writing from the University of Alaska Anchorage and lives in her hometown of Talkeetna, Alaska, with her canine friends, Jack Shephard and Lola Burger.